About the Author

I was born and raised in southern New Mexico and I now reside in Richmond, Virginia. I worked in factories and in construction most of my life and was in the Virginia Army National Guard for about fourteen years.

Sacrificale Grove
Hauntings

Larry Rhodes

Sacrificale Grove
Hauntings

Olympia Publishers
London

www.olympiapublishers.com
OLYMPIA PAPERBACK EDITION

Copyright © Larry Rhodes 2020

The right of Larry Rhodes to be identified as author of this work has been asserted in accordance with sections 77 and 78 of the Copyright, Designs and Patents Act 1988.

All Rights Reserved

No reproduction, copy or transmission of this publication may be made without written permission.
No paragraph of this publication may be reproduced, copied or transmitted save with the written permission of the publisher, or in accordance with the provisions of the Copyright Act 1956 (as amended).

Any person who commits any unauthorised act in relation to this publication may be liable to criminal prosecution and civil claims for damage.

A CIP catalogue record for this title is available from the British Library.

ISBN: 978-1-78830-709-3

This is a work of fiction.
Names, characters, places and incidents originate from the writer's imagination. Any resemblance to actual persons, living or dead, is purely coincidental.

First Published in 2020

**Olympia Publishers
Tallis House
2 Tallis Street
London
EC4Y 0AB**

Printed in Great Britain

Dedication

To Veronica who has been there from the beginning of the journey.

THE OLD HAUNT AND THE MISTY WOODS

Howdy and welcome to Sacrificale Grove. My name is George, by the way. I just stay in the guest house out behind this here mercantile with a couple of the other folks from the town. I can see by the look on your face that you're a bit confused. Never mind about that old path you're lookin' at; you don't want to cut through those woods north of here that's out by Clyde's old shack. You might think it's a short cut, but it ain't. Yep, there is a trail that leads into them woods. You can't see too much in there no how; it's always foggy in there. You go in there, you don't come back out. Even on the clearest of days, there is a thick foggy mist.

    It's said that them woods is haunted, but more likely they were cursed. No one really knows for sure. The woods surroundin' this here place consist of mostly birch and pine with a few oak trees here and there.

    Jimmie went into those woods of which he didn't believe in none of that mumbo jumbo superstition the older folks were tellin' him. They warned 'im. Many were scared to go near there but not Jimmie. He took that foot trail and never been seen or heard from since. There been some others who ventured up in that part of the woods but they weren't from around here; but then again, neither was Jimmie.

It's not natural the way the fog just lingers there. It doesn't move even when the wind blows through the trees. Heard some tell there's a chill in the air by some who came close to them. No, sir, they didn't stick around for long. They turned around and went back the way they came. Even the animals don't go in or near the place. Might catch a crow or a raven sittin' in one of the trees though.

Old Clyde built his shack where that old dirt road ends. Ayuh, next to the foot trail that leads into them fogged-over woods. Guess he tried to keep people from goin' into those woods after Jimmie disappeared. He acquired and took over a piece of land from the advice from someone he knew.

Some of them damn fools didn't listen to old Clyde. They thought he was pullin' their leg or somethin'. No, those people weren't from around here, no ways.

It was about fifty years ago that Clyde had that shack of his built. Heard Clyde tell he had seen a ghost or some such at the edge of those woods where it's fogged over. He said it looked like a spirit of a woman. He was no fool, weren't about to take that bait; he backed away real quick like and hid in his shack till daylight. He even had said that he heard a female's voice tryin' to entice him out. Clyde's place is empty now as he passed on some time ago.

T'ain't natural the way them trees are in that fog, all bare of leaves most of the year round. The trail looks overgrown when you first walk down it by old Clyde's abode with the trees in full bloom in the summer, then not long after, them birch and oak start to become barren of their leaves and of life. Even the pines lose their needles. That's when you start to feel that mist on your skin and the fog gets thicker the further you go in. Ain't no leaves on those trees from that point on, includin' the shrub that's out there. Yep, that's how Clyde put it.

Is that when Clyde saw that woman ghost or was that a different time? Well, he sure did see somethin' at one time or another. Anyways, that place may seem dead but there sure is somethin' in that part of the woods.

Old man Thomas and his spouse, Rebecca, set up a store at the crossroads on the north side of the main street next to that old dirt road that leads to Clyde's shack. That was before our time they got their mercantile built. You come across the store first way before you get to the township. The front door faces south; it seems fittin' as no one wants to be lookin' out toward the dead woods to the north.

Not natural that part of the woods with dead trees and such. Some folks who got close to that part of the woods mentioned seein' somethin', somethin' ghostly. But they didn't stay there long; they got out of there quick. Those folks seem to have a strong mind about them.

Frank was one of them folks who was up in that part of the woods, but he wasn't all that strong-minded. He didn't go up on that road towards Clyde's old place. He was out explorin' around that old haunt on the main thoroughfare up a ways from Thomas Mercantile, which also sits on the north side of the main road. You'll miss it if you don't know what you're lookin' for.

Frank didn't go inside that old house when he realized he was around it; he knew better from what he heard of the place. Besides, darn thing looks like it'll collapse in on itself. No, he went out behind that old haunt explorin'. He was lost in his own thoughts, the way he put it, when he realized somethin' was wrong. He felt a chill to the bones, and he stopped and looked about his surroundin's. He saw that he was at the edge of those forsaken misted woods, and he backed 'imself right out and as he did, he saw somethin' that scared 'im bad.

He wasn't able to describe what he saw though. Accordin' to Frank, it was like wakin' up from a bad nightmare. You know you dreamt somethin' bad but don't remember what you dreamt.

He left out of those woods headed straight to where he was livin' at, lookin' over his shoulder to make sure nothin' was followin' 'im. Whatever he saw in those woods spooked him bad.

Frank's doin' fine now, but don't see him out explorin' no more these days. He stays in the town mostly.

That old road up to Clyde's shack is about a mile long from Thomas Mercantile. It ends at a wall of birch, pine and lots of bushes and shrubbery. Mighty thick hedges grow there.

That part of the woods where the fog sits ain't natural. It's like bein' pulled and guided to them cursed woods. That's what Frank said at one time.

Somethin' queer about that old house that Frank was around that day. Should have collapsed a long time ago. Many people end up goin' crazy after bein' inside that old haunt. It's just up the road from Thomas Mercantile a bit before you get to Jacobs Tavern which Elizabeth runs. Those folks ended up dead not long after bein' in that old rot and ruin. Don't know how it's still standin' after all this time and the way it is.

Heard that somethin' happened in that old house long time ago, or so the rumor goes.

That house sits directly south of those misty dead woods. Don't really know when it was last occupied but heard from some of the older folks, not long after I got here, tell them folks who did live in there didn't last long in that house.

The way the story went, the husband killed 'imself and the missus went stir crazy before she died. Long time ago that happened. Mayhap over a hundred years ago. Do believe there is a remnant of another buildin' close to that old house. No one knows what it used to be, except for maybe some of the womenfolk in town.

You can say that old house is haunted. Even the land surroundin' the place is a little off. You could be lost in your own thoughts around the place, is how Frank put it. Won't know where you're goin' until it's too late.

Nature is coverin' the house up pretty good with all those vines and shrubs coverin' it all up. Like I said, you can miss it if you don't know what you're lookin' for. Looks like one of them homes from over three hundred years ago, just like some parts of the township itself.

Most folks ain't able to stay inside overnight if they manage to locate the place. You just might end up dead or disappear altogether.

It's not that bad durin' the daylight, but you don't wanna stay too long around that house. You'll start to see things: some ghostly images and hear some noises and voices out of nowhere.

Charley had been to that house at one time. He was skeptical when he heard some stuff about the place. Guess he just wanna check it out for 'imself. He had a strong mind about 'im. He checked out that old haunt way before Frank went explorin' near there. That was before Jimmie disappeared and Clyde had built his shack when Charley decided to investigate that place.

Charley spent at least two nights in the house. He had heard and seen things durin' that time that would make weak-minded folk go insane, or die of fright. There were a few times, mostly durin' the night he believed he dozed off and dreamt some disturbin' stuff, but did he really dream that stuff?

Believe it was Charley who found the remnant of the other buildin' that's close to the house. Charley thought he heard the laughter of children while checkin' the outside area around the house and the ruins he found. It was daylight when he heard the laughter echo through the surroundin' woods.

On the first night he spent in the old house, he heard what he described as a door to the outside crashin' open as if someone busted in and turned over some furniture, breakin' it up. He didn't understand how that was possible as there was no furniture anywhere and the door leadin' into the place was about rotted off. All the rooms were empty and what doors there was were rotted. He did check it out anyways to make sure no one else was there with him.

Durin' 'is stay there, he was supposed to have taken notes of what he witnessed and to this day no one knows what happened to 'em. It's like 'is notes vanished from the world.

I had wanted 'im to take some notes when I found out he was goin' to that old house. I sure didn't get a chance to read any of his notes before they disappeared.

Charley became a changed man after he stayed at the old haunt and he wasn't 'imself anymore. Sometime before he lost his mind, he had said that not only was the house haunted, it felt like it was cursed as well. He was never able to research the history of the house as there were no records bein' kept anywhere. Now there's a piece of history missin' around here and nobody knows nothin' about it as if nothin' happened at all.

Seems to be a connection between that old house and that part of the woods up north where that fog sits.

Charley had spotted some young folks the day after spendin' the first night in that desolate place. They were out behind the house away in the woods that surrounds the place. Them folks weren't from around here; they were from out of town. Seemed they had found an old footpath cuttin' through the birch wood out towards the misty woods. They never did see Charley out there as they were more focused on what they were lookin' at, or it could have been that they were lost in their own thoughts. Well, Charley did see that one of them was pointin' to somethin' on the forest floor that led to the house and another pointed off deeper in the woods and they were in some sort of discussion before they scampered off deeper into the woods. It was close to midday when that happened. It was at that time he had found the remnant of the other structure in the wooded area close to the old house. He almost tripped over the old ruin as the vegetation overtook it and there were quite a few oak trees surroundin' it as well. It appeared to be part of the terrain in that area.

Old Charley lost track of time that day and before he known it, the sun was dippin' on down to the western horizon.

He had no idea how he lost some of that time for he don't remember much of it or what he did for that matter.

Can't really track time in the township and the surroundin' area no how. Time has no meanin' here.

There was still plenty of daylight left for Charley though. He spotted some broken pieces of flagstone layin' about close by the back side of the house and around the ruins he had found. They appeared to lead into the woods where them young folks were at.

He went up to the place where he saw the group earlier, followin' a path of the flagstone fragments from the old house. Most of the stones were buried in the ground or covered over by fallen leaves over the years. The path led deeper into the woods with the fragments of the stones disappearin' all together with the trail bein' overgrown farther on. You wouldn't know if the path was there if you didn't know what to look for.

That house and the ruins along with the old trail that Charley discovered had a purpose in the old days, but most of the folks in the town knew nothin' about it, includin' Charley. Very few folks in town know, and they're keepin' it a secret.

As dusk was settlin' in, Charley went back to that old haunt to get ready for another night inside it, and once he got there, he heard rustlin' of leaves and twigs snappin' back in those woods. He also heard a faint frantic noise as if someone was urgin' another to keep goin' and the other was cryin' hysterically, just heedlessly runnin' through those woods. When Charley looked back, he saw a couple of those folks he had seen earlier that day runnin' out of the woods scared. Whatever there was deep in those woods spooked 'em real bad and them other folks were never seen again. Them two who came runnin' back never saw Charley or the house when they came out of them woods.

It was like they made a wide berth from where Charley was at, runnin' at full speed past those trees. He saw one, possibly the young man, tripped and fell face first then the young woman who was with him helped him back up and was gone.

Old Charley had a feelin' that what had happened had to do with the part of the woods that was fogged over. He soon heard the laughter of children out in those woods right after the couple ran out of there. Old Charley was disturbed by that as it sounded kind of evil. He knew them folks disappeared up in them woods just like the others before 'em. Ayuh, he stayed in the house that night as well, even though he felt uneasy about it.

You got to have a really strong mind to be able to stay there and come out alive like Charley did. May have to be brave or just a damn fool. There were times he had felt an urge to go up in those woods just like where them other folks went but he resisted that urge greatly to focus on his investigation.

Charley was tryin' to find out what the connection was between the old haunt and that fog in them woods up north was. While he was in one of the rooms upstairs, he had found a hidden compartment of which he found some old items and a crumblin' book that was wrapped in a tattered cloth. When he left that house, he took those items with 'im. Don't know what he ended up doin' with that stuff he found. He figured there could be a link that could tie them womenfolk to that house somehow. There was a small portrait that looked just like Jennifer that was among that old stuff. Charley knew there was somethin' off about some of them womenfolk but didn't know what that was until he started lookin' over what he found.

Most of them womenfolk of the township berated old Charley for stayin' at the old haunt when they found out what he did, tellin' 'im to leave well enough alone and not be snoopin' around like he was.

After Charley spent some time at the house, he sought out Clyde to inquire about them folks he had seen out in them woods behind that old haunt. Clyde told 'im that those young folks showed up in town on the day Charley went to the old house. Clyde saw Jennifer with them people, talkin' to 'em on a few occasions along with a couple of the other women. Clyde believed that those young folks were seduced by some of the women in town. He tried to get to them people to warn 'em, but Jennifer had a hold on 'em.

Them folks ended up leavin' out into those woods the next day after Jennifer got with them again.

Later that evenin', Clyde saw only two of them folks come out of the woods and they took off runnin' out towards the mercantile away from the township. Accordin' to Clyde, they seemed to be in fear for their lives.

Well, Clyde praised Charley for what he did and the knowledge he had found that some others didn't know. Jimmie didn't really believe in the mumbo jumbo that Charley was talkin' about. Most of it had to do with Jennifer seducin' Jimmie and whisperin' in his ear about things that no one else knew except for maybe some of the other womenfolk. She sure did have her way with Jimmie durin' his stay in that town.

No one talks about what happened durin' Charley's time in that house nowadays. Most of these folks in the town don't like people snoopin' around too much, especially those who are not from around these parts, for fear of the consequences most of the townfolks would face.

T'ain't natural the way Clyde and Charley passed on. No, don't believe they died a natural death. Well, Charley passed away after losin' his mind from stayin' in that old house. There were a few others like old Clyde and Charley, bein' renegades you might say, outlaws to the cause. They were tryin' to disrupt what them womenfolk been doin', with them seducin' those young folks who end up here in this place and castin' their magick. Some folks around these parts didn't care too much about 'em. Most of the womenfolk didn't like the way those fellows were doin'. No, sir, somethin' not natural with some of them womenfolk.

Don't see how that trail by Clyde's shack could be a short cut, no way. There's a river that flows southward near the town. That trail supposed to lead to the town common from Clyde's. Suppose to be a foot bridge where the trail ends to the river bank just a little north and to the west of the town. Can't really see that part of the river where that bridge is supposed to be as that fog sits there. The main bridge will get you to the township from the main thoroughfare. The town sits next to the river on the east side of it as soon as you cross that main bridge.

The township extends to the north some from that main road. On the northern side of the old town, vegetation grows thick as if it was a wall. Them townsfolks call that river Hallow Creek. There's a footpath that cuts through that vegetation up on the north end of the town close to where Hallow Creek flows due south. Just before you get to the river on that footpath, the vegetation seems to wilt and die away, leavin' only bare limbs of the birch and pine that grows there and the bushes around about, and you start to feel the dampness of that misty fog in them woods.

I had a peek up that path on the north end of town along with Allen when we were young lads. He and I ended up in this place as well. We got drawn in for some reason. Don't believe anyone remember Allen too much nowadays. Just before Allen went in deeper on that fogged-over trail, he called me a chickenshit 'cause I didn't want to go any farther. I lost sight of Allen 'cause that fog was so thick the further Allen went and I never did go in after 'im.

I was leery of those woods because I known some folks went up in them and never came back, and I heard some of the stories from those who got close to that part of the woods. What happened to Allen was years before Jimmie disappeared up in the woods out by Clyde's old shack. Even I tried to warn Jimmie about them woods and about some of them womenfolk, but all for naught.

I sure saw somethin' in that fog when Allen left me standin' there but I wouldn't talk about it none.

No one really talks about them folks who went into them wicked woods but if they did, they did it in hushed tones so's not to be overheard by some they didn't want them to know what they were talkin' about.

Heard there was an old cemetery up in those woods where that fog sits. Not too sure though as nobody came back to verify that claim.

It was purdy bad for the folks here in this area before Thomas and Rebecca had their shop set up. People were disappearin' more then, than now. That fog just crept right out of them woods at night. Many folks back then stayed indoors durin' that time. Those who were caught outside were never seen again. At the first light of dawn that fog retreated back into them woods. Story was that the fog came out of the ground from that old cemetery, as the rumor was anyways back in them days.

You don't wanna be around this place on old hollow's eve or what some of the folks here call it "Samhain". You best be indoors durin' that time of the year.

The place for a newcomer to stay is at Jacobs Tavern that sits on the west side of Hallow Creek, on the south side of the main road.

Those spirits tend to come out of that misty fog at that time and a mist covers the earth floor. Those ghosts try to entice folks around here to follow 'em right out to those woods where they came from. T'ain't natural the way they call your name and not hearin' no one else's. Then the laugh you hear later don't sound evil, but seductive, and you might catch a giggle here or there, like a seductive woman might do.

Suppose that's what happened to those folks who disappeared in them woods, hearin' their name bein' called out seductively with that laughter shortly thereafter.

Frank had said that it wasn't just the chill in the air that stopped him in his tracks, it was also someone or somethin' had called out his name from those woods.

Some of them womenfolk may know what's goin' on but they're not talkin' none. The menfolk in these parts may think they're in charge, but they ain't.

Frank don't look at some of them womenfolk like he used to. He cast his eyes downward or look elsewhere while he's in their presence.

Rebecca outlived her husband, Thomas, and do believe it was her idea to set up the mercantile where it's at now. No one ever talks about the time before Rebecca and Thomas set up the store. Them folks all died away who lived back in those days. They all took some secret they knew to their grave, so to speak.

Some of the womenfolk in the township may know what that secret may be, but they ain't tellin'.

Elizabeth may know what that secret may have been – you can see it in her eyes; she runs Jacobs Tavern, providin' newcomers a room to stay in.

Clyde had a fallin' out with one of the womenfolk, do believe it was Jennifer. He blamed her for Jimmie's foolishness of goin' up into them misty woods.

Most folks in this area are a little peculiar; they ain't right the way they are.

Most newcomers don't stay around too long after they get here. Very few brave souls stick around and try to make it their home like Frank did. Not many people come to this place nowadays, not like they use to back in the old days. Some of them people who come to this place think they can just pass through until they find out there's no outlet except the way they came in.

Jimmie wasn't from around these parts. He was one of them newcomers of which he liked what he saw in this place, so he stayed and made it his home. T'others didn't see what Jimmie saw in that old town. Most of them other folks saw somethin' else. Well, Jimmie really wasn't the superstitious type of a feller.

There's a schoolhouse on up aways, after you cross the main bridge that spans Hallow Creek. It ain't all that big though, and there ain't many school-age kids in town.

It's mostly the young folks who end up in this place go into those woods on the north end. They could be adventure seekers, but not likely.

That old road that goes up to Clyde's place don't get used much anymore as nature is tryin' to take it back.

Frank knows some things about those woods and about some of the folks here in this area but he dare not say nothin' about any of it 'cause he has to be careful of what he says, especially around some of the womenfolk. He gets real quiet around them. He may have seen somethin' he weren't suppose to have seen. The looks he gets from some of them women says 'You best not say nothin' if you know what's good for you.'

Those birch and pine look more like skeletal figures standin' out there in that fog in the woods and you could swear that they move sometimes. That's what George had said at one time to try to keep Jimmie from goin' in there. George noticed that Jimmie was a lot like Allen in many ways.

There's a novelty-style mercantile near the town common which seems out of place as the township don't get no tourists, just mostly folks who seem lost as at to where they are. Susan Moore runs the little store, invitin' all newcomers in. Try not to go in if you can help it. Strange name for a novelty store, bein' called Damnosus Gifts, if you know what I mean.

Some of the folks in this place are a little strange to tell the truth. The way some of them look at the newcomers, t'ain't natural. Some of the folks in the town seem younger than their true age when you first look to 'em. You can tell they're older by the look in their eyes. It's mainly them women, they don't seem normal at all. It's like they are lookin' into your soul with those eyes of theirs. Guess that's why Frank averts his eyes when he's around some of them womenfolk.

Don't think things were like they are nowadays as they were a long time ago. They were a little worse then. Maybe a couple hundred years ago that was, not sure exactly when though. Somethin' happened then, but no one knows today. Some of them women may know what had happened, but they ain't tellin'. They're very secretive of the past and very mysterious. It's got to have somethin' to do with them woods up to the north, the way they are all foggy and such.

Old Clyde really wasn't too comfy stayin' in the township, feelin' uneasy bein' around the womenfolk and all. Guess that's part of the reason why Clyde built his shack where it is, aside from what happened to Jimmie. He also tried to keep out-of-towners from goin' into those woods on his end but couldn't do nothin' about the path on the town side.

This here little town looks deserted when you first get to it. Ayuh, seems to be abandoned until you get a closer look. Then the place gotcha. Sure ain't natural the town is, just like them woods. The old buildin's look like empty husks, no life in 'em at first glance. You might see Frank out and about, sometimes workin' or fixin' on somethin'. He's now the local handyman in these parts and almost as if he's the only livin' person around, but don't let that fool ya. Some folks around here don't really care for newcomers comin' around here, so they're not so quick to show themselves.

This is the end of my tale for now. You take care and don't let them women seduce you. Keep a strong mind about you. See you in the morrow, if you're still here that is, and I'll tell you some more of the story of this place. Do try to stay out of them woods.

A WARM WELCOME...

OR NOT

Welcome back, I see that you survived your first night here in this place. I hope you slept well in Jacobs Tavern, if that's where you went. As you already know, this place ain't easy to find, and you won't find it on any known map. It's one of those places that you might accidently come across. Don't think anybody knows of this place but maybe a handful, if that. Those who have come here don't really know how they came to be here. Most said they came through some thick fog while travelin' on an old country road and while they were goin' through that fog, there were no turn-offs at all.

It wouldn't matter if it was day or night, rain or shine, if those folks got caught in that unusual fog, they end up in this place. Those young folks had said that the fog was so thick, they couldn't see but just a couple of feet ahead of 'em, and it's worse at night.

Don't really know if those who left from this place ever made it back to where they came from. Some of the others who came here got pulled into those woods.

That old road is the only one in and out of this place of which you'll reach the Thomas Mercantile first. A lot of the people who end up here never notice the old house set back in the woods when they continue on up the main dirt road. A little further down past that old haunt is Jacobs Tavern next to the main bridge spannin' Hallow Creek leadin' into the town.

Most of the folks who end up at this place tend to have a look of confusion, wonderment and fascination, and wondered how this town got to be here or how they themselves got to be here 'cause this here place was never where them folks were from, of what they had said.

There is a wooden sign off to the side of the main road as soon as you come out of that fog. It's so faded you can barely read what's on it and know what it says anymore, and it looks like it's been there forever.

Not many people come to this place anymore like there use to be before Rebecca and Thomas got their mercantile goin'.

The town and surroundin' area got cut off from the rest of the world a long time ago. May have somethin' to do with that fog those young folks has to pass through just while bein' led here. There ain't nothin' here for them people these days now. Nope, this here place doesn't have no such technologies that them folks talk about when they get here nowadays. They do complain that their gadgets don't work and soon find out there's no electricity at all in these parts. Yep, it's a dead-end place of which them folks should've turnt around and went back to where they had come from. Old Clyde been known to say that, and I would agreed with 'im, that's if they were able to get back to where they did come from that is.

Clyde, Charley and I tried to get them young folks who came to this place to turn around and head back the way they came. Most of the local folks in the town didn't like what those men were doin', even if some of 'em didn't care for the newcomers comin' into the township.

Most of these local folks in town claimed it was the Rites that had the newcomers come to this place and be drawn to the part of the woods where that fog just sits. Those people who came here didn't know anythin' about that at all until it was too late.

Those few who sensed somethin' was wrong treaded lightly in them woods up north of here and when they saw what was up, they got out of that place quick and knew the true nature of this here town, Ayuh, they had left from this place in a hurry of which I would like to believe they had made it back to where they came from. Never knew for certain though.

Most likely some of them womenfolk had people like Clyde done away with and made it out like a natural death, but don't believe it was.

Not many people come to this place anymore like they use to and do believe Thomas or Rebecca had somethin' to do with that. Well, this here mercantile really weren't suppose to be where it is now. There is already a store in the town itself but it's more like a novelty shop.

Some of those women in the town was very suspicious of what Rebecca and Thomas were doin': the couple gettin' their store built out of town next to the path that led up to Clyde's shack. No sooner they had it built, the amount of people comin' here was cut back dramatically. Thomas passed away sometime after the mercantile opened and don't really know what became of Rebecca.

This whole place has that ancient feel to it. It starts to weigh on you the more you spend your time here. It's like steppin' in a dead past when you get to this place. You probably get the feelin' this here township ain't got no soul to it as most of the folks around here, but some of them people are alive in a way.

Those people who end up in this here place don't see anyone at all at first. It's like arrivin' at one of those ghost towns them young folks had talked about. The folks around here won't let them newcomers see 'em unless they want to be seen.

Samantha runs Thomas Mercantile now. Do believe she's Rebecca's granddaughter or great-granddaughter, don't know which for sure, but she sure looks just like Rebecca in a lot of ways and also bein' colored as well. Could swear they could be twins.

Some of them young folks who ended up in this place stopped at this here store first, seein' that it was the only buildin' those people saw after travelin' through that fog for quite a while. Some others took that old road up to Clyde's, since that is the only turn off here. Maybe they hoped the road would lead 'em where they wanted to go, but it dead-ended up ahead, so them folks had to come back to the main thoroughfare and this here mercantile. There were a few who didn't turn around when they got to Clyde's old shack and they ended up goin' into those woods followin' that footpath up there, they did. A lot of 'em kept on goin' down the main road to the tavern and the town itself. Ohh, a few do come back to Thomas Mercantile.

Those who stopped in here at the mercantile notices that the place has no refrigerated ice box for cold stuff, Whatever that is, or any kind of electronic gadgets, whatever they may be, but they do see some dry food stuff and some garden-grown vegetables and odds and ends that country folks around here may need.

It sure do appear that the newcomers stepped right into the past from their perspective.

Samantha would greet them folks kindly and informs them that the town up ahead is just a dead end with no other way out except the way they came in, and it's just a dead old ghost town, which there's nothin' there for them folks at all, so them folks just might as well turn around and head on back the way they came and not to be takin' that old path next to the store; it just ends about a mile down there with no way out, nothin' for sure that way.

Most of them folks ended up headin' into the town anyways. Guess they felt compelled to go there, mayhap drawn into it for some reason, or it was just callin' to 'em.

Few of t'other folks took heed of what Samantha had said and left out back where they came from. Not too sure if they made it back or not, no word on that at all.

***

Some of the womenfolk in the town ain't too concerned about those dead woods of where them foot trails lead. Accordin' to them there ain't nothin' wrong with those woods at all. Some of them womenfolk are a little peculiar and somethin' ain't natural about 'em if the truth be known. Don't seem like they're afraid of them fogged-over woods like some of the other folks around these parts are.

Those women sure do have a look about 'em that says 'come hither, I won't bite' type look. Anyone with a good strong mind would know there's somethin' not right about that look.

Them women don't go to Thomas Mercantile that Samantha runs. They have an evil look about 'em when they look out toward this here store. Somethin' about it them women don't like at all. Can't say for certain what that could be but Thomas and Rebecca might have known somethin' about what that could be but they ain't around no more.

Some of them womenfolk don't like to show off their true form as they like what they're showin' t'others. Yep, they sure do like showin' other people what they used to look like back in them old days. Guess those women don't want to scare off the newcomers too soon.

Some of the folks with a strong mind who ended up here sensed somethin' was wrong, but they didn't find out what it was until it was too late.

Most folks around here don't come out to be seen by out-of-towners, but they would if it played to their advantage like Elizabeth. She would show herself to those people who get drawn into this place as most of them folks end up goin' into Jacobs Tavern seekin' shelter for the night, that's if they hadn't gone anywhere else that is. Even if those folks had gone somewhere else durin' the day, they end up at Jacobs Tavern nonetheless as the entrance is always open to anybody.

That damn place looks abandoned at first glance, like an empty shell, but it sure is invitin' to those out in the cold and rain, which it makes for good shelter for those seekin' it. There ain't never a fire in the hearth of which that large fireplace is located off to the left on the far wall of the common room when you enter the premise.

The tavern seems to be empty of life when you first enter the place, and then Elizabeth appears from the darkness of the shadows bearin' a single lit candle of which it illuminates her pale complexion and blood-red lips. Of what you might be able to tell she ain't too slender body-wise, wearin' a dark dress.

Elizabeth will greet ya with a seductive smile and bid you welcome and offer you a room for the night while assurin' that there's nothin' to fear.

There's somethin' odd about that tavern from what was told by some folks who had been there before. While the whole place, inside and out, looks really rustic with age, the furnishin's in the bedrooms are newly polished wood and the beddin' is very clean, includin' the linens.

Those floorboards in the tavern and many of the other buildin's in the town would creak and groan with protest as you walk upon 'em. You got to use candles to see by in those dark rooms up in that tavern.

Don't really know how those folks slept in that place as some of 'em must have had a fitful night with disturbin' dreams 'cause you could see it in their eyes. They must have been too scared or too embarrassed to mention what they had dreamt. Possibly, they don't remember but known they had a disturbin' dream while they slept in one of the rooms in that there tavern.

You'll see Frank out and about workin' on one of the old buildin's in town just like some of the other folks who had come before. You won't see Elizabeth very much out in town, but she sure will be seein' you and the other folks who would come to this place. Frank will talk some but he's very careful of what he says and pretty sure, deep down inside of 'imself, he wants to tell them folks who comes here to get out of this place and not to look back and damn sure tell 'em to not go up in those woods north of here, no matter how strong the temptation may be. Well, he dare not say nothin' like that for he knows what would happen to 'im if he does.

Susan Moore runs the local novelty mercantile, Damnosus Gifts. Now she would appear to the newcomers when she sees fit, and she sure has a way about her to get them folks into her shop.

The schoolhouse ain't that far from that novelty store. Most of them folks who just enter that town won't notice the few children that are at that school 'cause those tykes love to play games on 'em, and them games ain't playful silly games neither.

Susan ain't just seductive to the men, but to the other women who end up in township as well. She sure can get them folks to accept a gift from her store by havin' them choose one item only. She just might be a little generous to the outsiders and givin' 'em a warm welcome into the town, but not likely.

It's those folks' choice if they want to take the gift or not, but my opinion, they shouldn't take it no way if them folks knew what those gifts were. Most of them folks end up takin' a gift anyways. Those items are more like a cursed charm than anythin' else. Each of them charms calls out to whoever they want to be with somehow.

The young folks who come here with a strong mind could tell there's somethin' wrong with those items that Susan is tryin' to give 'em, but them folks can't really put a finger on what that could be. Some of them strong-minded folks end up takin' a charm, I'm guessin' they didn't want to be rude, whereas others left those charms alone.

The longer them folks stay here in this township and the surroundin' area, the more likely they would want to check out them woods north of here. Those cursed charms and Susan's enticement makes them folks have a stronger urge to go into them woods.

Some of the womenfolk in town are suspicious of those strong-minded people who happened to end up here with the other young folks. Those type of people sure do get the feelin' somethin' ain't right here in this place the longer they stay in this forsaken area.

Victoria takes care of the few children that are here in town at the schoolhouse of which she has that air of authority about her. She doesn't care too much about them outsiders, but she follows the Rite and tolerates them folks.

Those kids in this here township don't seem to be right at all. There's somethin' that ain't natural about them little buggers. Seems like they can be a little devilish at times. Those little heathens have a knack of laughin' and gigglin' which seemed to be the same kind of laughter that Charley had heard while he was at that old haunt. They may be very mischievous, but they don't act out in the presence of Victoria. You can hear them little tykes most of the time but you won't see 'em. They can give off a vibe of bein' a little too creepy to some folks.

There are times when some of those out-of-towners come to this place, they don't see anyone outside and the buildin's in the town appear to be just silent shells sittin' around. When them folks cross that bridge spannin' Hallow Creek, one or two of 'em might hear the laughter of a child somewhere in that town.

Those folks who heard that laughter will try to get the others who are with 'em to go where they had heard that laugh came from. Sometimes those folks might catch sight of a small figure run around the corner of one of them buildin's in that town. Damn fools won't see nothin' when they get to where they saw that figure run to, and then some of those folks would hear some laughter and gigglin' from some of the other children. You may never know where they may be until you spot one or two of those little bastards. It's like playin' cat and mouse with those kids.

Eventually those little devils will lead them folks who are chasin' after 'em to that foot path that cuts into that thick vegetation north of town. That trail supposed to go up to Hallow Creek just a little north of the town where a foot bridge supposed to be, but you won't see it 'cause of that misty fog up in those woods of which you will run into first. When they had gotten to that place on the trail, some of those folks had heard their name whispered out to 'em. Yep, those people fell for that trick those kids played on 'em and some of those folks end up goin' deeper down that path in that thick fog, never to be seen again. Some of the strong-minded folks will sense somethin' wrong after a while and they won't continue playin' that game no more.

There are other times them kids will lead them young folks on toward that old haunt and into the woods in that direction north of that haunted house. That could be what happened to them folks who Charley saw while he was around that place some years ago.

Those kids love to split them out-of-towners in different directions if there's more than three who end up in this here place sometimes.

The children here in this township sure ain't afraid of those woods up north or what could be in 'em. Mayhap them kids came from that cursed place in the woods, but don't really know that for sure though.

Victoria is the only person who can handle those kids. Frank don't mess with them children 'cause he knows what they are and do believe he knows what some of them women are too.

Damn shame about some of the other folks who use to live here in this township. Not many of 'em were able to leave from here. Frank stay in the town with a few more other folks who ain't like some of those womenfolk. Patti used to stay in the town but she now stays in the guest house behind this here mercantile. The womenfolk like Victoria and Elizabeth made those other folks avoid the outsiders as much as possible with the exception of Frank. Those other folks in town don't really want to end up like Clyde and the others of his kind.

Frank does help out Elizabeth at Jacobs Tavern sometimes. You can say that some of them folks in town could be servants to some of those wicked women.

Well, I'm done for now 'cause I'm a little tired. Old age is catchin' up to me. Come back in the morrow if ya want to know about Jimmie and his disappearance, and a little bit more about this here place.

Take care of yourself and don't accept anythin' from Susan and stay clear of them creepy kids in town.

THE TAKING OF JIMMIE

Mornin', hope your stay here is unforgettable. You don't seem to be lookin' too good. Are you sleepin' well? You kind of look like you may have seen a ghost or somethin'. Hope you stayed away from those little imps masqueradin' as kids like I told ya.

Well, I'm pretty sure you seen them young folks who had came into this place just like you did. They showed up shortly after you left yesterday and, no, I haven't seen 'em since then. Hope they didn't get lured up into those woods I told you about.

Anyways, since you're here, I'm guessin' you want to know a little more about what happened to Jimmie.

I'll tell ya this, Clyde's old shack is gonna collapse if nobody fixes it up as it was built about fifty years ago. Clyde was one of those folks who had a strong mind about 'em. Some of those womenfolk weren't too thrilled with old Clyde. He started speakin' his mind and started to be resistant of them women.

Them evil women didn't have too much power over Clyde. He was bold enough to get some of them outsiders to turn around and leave this area, he sure did. Jennifer wasn't too proud of what Clyde was doin'. She and some of the other women did what they could to keep Clyde under their control, but he was persistent though.

Jimmie had showed up one day and he was a little bewildered by what he saw here. He's been all over those old country roads where he had came from and never had he happened on a place like this here township, but then he never been through no thick fog like he did either. He thought of that fog as some kind of freak of nature that the weather does sometimes, just like how a tornado would skip one house and destroy the others around it.

Jimmie sure wasn't into no superstitious crap like some other people may be.

He didn't have no other place to go and had no kin folk who would miss 'im, so he figured he would make this here place a home for 'imself.

That boy sure was real down to earth and got along with just about everyone he met in this area, but he wasn't all that strong-minded even though he had some wits about 'im. Some of them womenfolk tried to entice Jimmie to go into them woods up north, but he kept puttin' 'em off 'cause there were so many other stuff he wanted to check out and do first while he was here in this township.

Old Clyde tried to get Jimmie to leave out from this area and go back where he came from, but Jimmie just didn't want to leave as he liked livin' up in that town. I saw a lot of Allen in Jimmie, maybe that's why I was taken in by the boy. I even tried to pass on word to Jimmie to not listen to some of them womenfolk and it would be best for Jimmie to leave out from this here township, but Jimmie wasn't about to have all that nonsense about leavin' from here as it was now his home.

After I took Jimmie under his wings, Clyde started to be taken in by the boy, but he didn't let that be known to anyone as old Clyde didn't want to be seen as bein' soft and kindhearted. Some of them womenfolk weren't likin' the idea of me and the others givin' Jimmie guidance too much as they felt them men were messin' with the Rites.

Even Charley was talkin' some common sense to the boy and Jimmie was startin' to take in what those men were tellin' 'im. He was tellin' them men that he would be careful and for 'em not to worry so much.

Well, Jennifer did manage to seduce Jimmie sometime later, whisperin' somethin' into his ear, but don't rightly know what it was she had said to 'im. Maybe it was a promise of some kind of treat from her that only grown folks are likely to be doin'. She sure was tryin' to put her spell on 'im but those men were doin' their best to undo her hold on the boy, and they tried as much as they could to break that spell she was weavin'.

Jennifer did finally manage to get her spell worked on Jimmie despite what those men were tryin' to do to undo her work. Ayuh, she got the boy to believe there was nothin' wrong with those woods up north as opposed to what some others may have told 'im. With him not all that superstitious anyways, he was havin' a hard time believin' that there was somethin' wrong with them woods. He did say to those guys that he was gonna show 'em that there was nothin' to be scared of in them woods one day.

Seemed like Jimmie was struck by love with Jennifer and he had that certain glow about 'im when he was around her with that smile splayed on his face. It could have been lust. the way he looked at her sometimes of which it may have been what she was whisperin' to 'im. There sure was no love on Jennifer's end though; she just used that affection to her advantage.

One day Jimmie decided to sneak off out of town shortly after Jennifer had whispered somethin' in his ear, then she put her lips on his, givin' Jimmie a soft kiss. It appeared to be a lovin' kiss while she had the palm of her hand on his lower cheek close to the jawline to anyone who would be witnessin' it, but it was more likely the kiss of death if you ask me.

No one rightly knows what Jennifer said to Jimmie but whatever she had told 'im sure did have 'im excited about whatever it was.

Old Clyde spotted them two together out by the old stable that's next to Damnosus Gifts, or is it an old barn?' He had seen that kiss Jennifer gave to the boy. Just after she kissed Jimmie, Jennifer turned her head slightly and looked straight at Clyde with a smirk as if she knew exactly where he was at.

Clyde knew then there weren't nothin' right about what Jennifer was doin', and when Jimmie snuck off shortly after, old Clyde followed 'im, keepin' some distance back.

Jimmie went on up the main dirt road towards Thomas Mercantile crossin' the bridge spannin' Hallow Creek, and passin' the tavern and that old house off in the woods on the north side of the road. When he reached this here store, Jimmie cut to the back side of the buildin' goin' on that there old dirt trail to where it ends up a mile back there.

It seemed to Clyde that Jimmie wasn't too concerned about who, if anyone, was followin' him 'cause he never did look back behind 'im to see if there was anybody followin' him. Well, Clyde did stay far enough back to be sure that Jimmie wouldn't know that he was bein' followed.

Jimmie made it to the end of that road after a while, while Clyde stuck to the side of the road near them birch trees and bushes away from them cursed woods.

While Jimmie was standin' near the wall of trees and bushes at the end of the old dirt road and close by the foot trail that led off to the east, Clyde eased 'imself closer to where the boy was at, stayin' hidden' in the woods as not to be seen, all the while wonderin' what the hell that foul woman told Jimmie.

Old Clyde figured that Jimmie was waitin' for somethin' or someone the way the boy was lookin' down the road toward Thomas Mercantile and lookin' towards that footpath, expectin' somethin'.

After Jimmie had been out there for quite a while, he started to get a little antsy, runnin' his hands through 'is hair while pacin' some from one side of the road to the other lookin' somewhat gloomy as if he had the feelin' of bein' let down.

Clyde didn't feel any kind of way about the situation; he was just hopin' that Jimmie wouldn't take that foot trail into them cursed woods where that fog is. He may have been a little gruff with Jimmie at times but he did care enough about the boy that he didn't want nothin' bad to happen to 'im.

Clyde thought that Jimmie was gonna leave that area and head back to town, as the boy started to walk back down the road, then Jimmie stopped next to that trail, peerin' through the woods that the path cuts through, beamin' with joy and speakin' to someone who Clyde wasn't able to see from his vantage point, but he had to have known that somebody was on that trail.

Just from the way Jimmie was smilin', bein' all bashful lookin' and havin' a radiant glow about 'im, Clyde knew then who it could have been down on that footpath, 'cause that was how Jimmie reacted when he was around Jennifer all those times before. What Clyde didn't understand was how she got to that part of the woods when neither he nor Jimmie saw her walkin' up that old dirt road they both took, unless Jennifer went through them cursed fogged-over woods from that trail off on the north end of town somehow.

Clyde known right then that somethin' was really wrong about the whole situation, but he wasn't able to move or speak out to warn Jimmie at all but was just only able to watch as the events unfolded before 'im. He felt like he was under some sort of spell as if someone or somethin' had cast some kind of magick on 'im.

From the way Jimmie acted, inchin' his way toward that foot trail, it looked like to Clyde that the boy was lovestruck and Clyde wasn't able to do anythin' about it to keep the boy from goin' on that path at all.

Clyde then saw her slither her way on out of the woods more in the open to where he could see her on that footpath. Clyde noticed that she wasn't wearin' what she had on earlier that day but what looked like an old night gown that women use to wear back about two hundred years ago or so, and down near her feet the garment was frayed and tattered.

It appeared that Jennifer had a warm sweet smile for Jimmie but that didn't fool old Clyde none. The color of her lips was blood-red of what Clyde could tell.

She reached out and took Jimmie's hand in hers, then looked straight dead into Clyde's eye's, displayin' a smirk, just like she did before, while turnin' around to lead the dumbfounded boy into those accursed woods. Clyde figured somethin' ain't natural by the way that woman knew where he was hidin' when she looked at 'im. It was like she was lookin' into his soul. Sure do believe that she did that deliberately just to show Clyde that she can do whatever she wants and there ain't nothin' he or any other can do about it.

That foul woman then led Jimmie into those accursed woods while Clyde tried to summon all his willpower to break out of that bond that he was put in, and he finally did manage to break free and, when he did, he gave chase crossin' the road to that trail to try to get to Jimmie before the boy fell victim to them misty woods.

As soon as Clyde got on the footpath chasin' after Jimmie, he started trippin' over what looked like roots comin' out of the ground as he ran as best he could. It seemed like somethin' was tryin' to keep 'im from reachin' Jimmie out on that trail. Even the tree limbs from those birch and few pine trees were grabbin' at old Clyde as if they had long fingers with sharp nails reachin' out toward 'im with those leaves, of what was left of them leaves at that time, slappin' at old Clyde. All the while Clyde was hollerin' out after Jimmie for 'im to come back and not to go into that fog that's in them woods.

It appeared that the vegetation around that trail that Clyde was on had grown thick with long grass and weeds while he was out there that day when normally there weren't that much to begin with.

As Clyde went further in them woods, the landscape around him changed abruptly with the vegetation dyin' away and those birch trees and bushes became nothin' but skeletal remains. Even those few evergreen trees lost their needles, leavin' them bare.

Just past where that vegetation died away, you could see wisps of fog swirlin' around and you start to feel that moisture in the air which gives off that rotten feel in the air. That was how Clyde put it when he got to that point of which he halted in his tracks and wouldn't dare go in any further as that fog got thicker in them woods and he knew that he would end up with the same fate as the others who had gone in there.

Ayuh, that fog sure do get a lot thicker the farther you look in those woods and you're not able to tell if there are any more trees, bushes or anythin' else further on up in there.

The fog wasn't that thick where Clyde was standin' while he was lookin' around to see if he could spot Jimmie somewhere around that area. Well, he sure did spot somethin' alright, and just a few feet into that dead place in front of Clyde she materialized out of that fog as if she was a part of that dreaded stuff itself.

Old Clyde thought that it was Jennifer comin' out of that foggy mist wearin' that night gown he had seen on her earlier, but now it was more dingy and tattered than before, showin' more of the woman's flesh and one of her breasts was fully exposed, and she seemed to be ethereal 'cause Clyde was able to see through the woman.

Just as that woman came out of that fog and got closer to Clyde, the skin and tissue of her bottom half of her face came peelin' off from the nose to the chin, showin' bone and her teeth, and her eyes turned coal black.

Clyde just stared wide eye at the horror he was seein' before 'im and didn't have the willpower to move for a moment 'cause of the fright that was coursin' through 'im.

Then that monstrosity began to open its mouth and, as it did, its mouth started to transform into somethin' more grotesque with fangs like a vampire's, if you believe in such things, but the facial area was a little more deformed to where you couldn't tell if it was like a vampire or somethin' else.

All the while that thing was openin' its mouth, there was a hissin' growl comin' out from its face, if you can call it that, and then there was an unnatural shriek just when the thing's mouth was about fully open.

There was somethin' that brought Clyde's mind back to what was happenin', and he sure didn't stay there where he was. He back-pedaled, tripped and fell on his ass, but that didn't stop 'im none. He managed to get 'imself back on his feet quickly and got out of them woods as fast as he could, and was stumblin' on those roots that had came out of the earth on the trail he was followin', tryin' to get back to that old road.

Clyde came out of those woods off that footpath and onto that road headin' back to Thomas Mercantile and he could still hear that growl and unnatural shriek in his head. While he was makin' that one-mile trek back to the store, Clyde thought he had heard a woman's laughter comin' out of those woods off to his left of where that misty fog sits.

By the time Clyde got to the mercantile, he could feel his heart thumpin' in his chest and he was covered in sweat. There he met up with me and Charley as we were sittin' on the porch of this here store talkin' amongst each other.

Well, Thomas Mercantile does seem to be like a safe haven for those regular folks who live in the town for some reason or another.

Charley inquired about what got Clyde all rattled and he told 'em what went down earlier that day and how Jimmie ended up in those woods north of the store where they were at.

Yep, old Clyde knew somethin' wasn't right with some of those folks here in this township, but he wasn't expectin' what he witnessed.

With Clyde mentionin' that it was Jennifer who had led Jimmie up in those woods, Charley spoke up and said that it couldn't have been her 'cause he and several others had seen the woman around town the whole day and them two men just got to the mercantile when Clyde showed up all flustered, and I agreed with that 'cause I'd seen Jennifer myself.

After Clyde heard what was told to 'im by those men, he had a dumbfound confused look about 'im and his jaw was a little slack 'cause he couldn't believe what he heard from those two guys for he sworn that was Jennifer he had seen who led Jimmie up in those woods on that foot trail.

Many of the other folks in the town would disagree with Clyde on him seein' Jennifer where he said she was 'cause they had also seen her around town the whole day, even had seen her with Jimmie earlier that day as well.

Well. Clyde sure wasn't' satisfied with the news he had received so he hitched up his courage and he went to confront Jennifer 'isself and boldly strode into town lookin' for the monstrosity of a woman that she was, accordin' to Clyde.

He caught up with that woman by the old tool shop that the blacksmith was attached to, which wasn't too far from the novelty mercantile. That tool shop is where Frank spends most of his time nowadays and you can reach it quickly after you cross that main bridge spannin' Hallow Creek on the north side of the main dirt road.

There's some stables or a small barn sittin' between the blacksmith shop and Damnosus Gifts as you turn off the main dirt road goin' to the northern part of the town. The furnace and kiln in the blacksmith don't get used much anymore these days.

As Clyde was walkin' up towards her near the tool shop, he declared loudly that he knew what she was, and he didn't care if anybody else was listenin' to what he had to say either. He accused Jennifer and some of the other womenfolk she been around of doin' magick and spellwork to fool the folks here in town and those who end up in this place, and puttin' a spell on Jimmie to make 'im go off in them woods like he did.

He sure didn't get up too close to that woman for he didn't know what she would do to him at that time, and he dared not get close to her at all.

While Clyde was layin' on the accusations on Jennifer, a few of them womenfolk who were in league with her was standin' stone-cold silent with no emotions whatsoever. The other folks in town who heard what Clyde was sayin' couldn't believe what they heard.

She said with a smirk, "Why, Clyde, whatever do you mean?"

"You know damn well what I mean."

Yep, there were some foul words that Clyde spoke to Jennifer and he didn't care who heard any of it, and after speakin' what he wanted to say to the woman, he turned away from her and left. After he left, those other womenfolk who stood there silently lookin' at Clyde went right back to what they were doin' with a warm smile as if there was nothin' wrong at all or what transpired never happened.

Some of them other folks who overheard what was said were stunned for a little while and they were expectin' somethin' to happen to Clyde while he walked away with his back toward Jennifer, but nothin' ever happened as she just let 'im go.

Well, Clyde decided to walk back to Thomas Mercantile where Charley and I were at 'cause that is where he felt the safest.

Charlene Roberta, bein' the daughter of Rebecca and Thomas, took over Thomas Mercantile and she was runnin' the store at the time Jimmie disappeared in those woods up north. Seems mighty strange that Charlene looked just like Rebecca. It must be a family trait.

Charlene had heard about what Clyde had said to Jennifer by one of the folks who had came by her shop and had already known what went down between Clyde and Jennifer. Do believe it was Charlene's idea that Clyde should go on and take over part of the land at the end of that old dirt road leadin' up north of Thomas Mercantile and build 'imself a place up there where it ends as he wasn't too keen on goin' back into that town.

Well, Clyde wasn't too sure about goin' back up that old road after what he had been through, but Charlene reassured 'im that things would be alright and she passed to him a charm bag and instructed Clyde to bury it under his home when he got it built.

When she gave Clyde the charm bag and after hearin' what she instructed 'im to do with it, he got real suspicious of the thing and of her of which made 'im wonder about the woman, and she then immediately informed 'im that she wasn't like Jennifer or some of the other women back in the town itself. Charlene pointed out to 'im that those type of folks have never came near the mercantile at all but only go as far as that tavern that's close to the town. It was only the folks like him who are able to come to her store at all with nothin' to fear about the place.

"Well, doesn't it feel like a safe haven for you or not?" Charlene posed that question for Clyde to mull over for a little while.

After thinkin' it over, Clyde's mind was put at ease a little bit but not much as he still was wonderin' what kind of secrets she was keepin', but he did do what she instructed 'im to do, and that shack of his is still standin' right where he built it with that charm bag buried underneath.

Several months after Clyde finished buildin' his new home, he had seen what looked like a spirit of a woman up in those woods where that trail is at, and she was floatin' about as if she was part of some mist or fog. At that time when he seen the ghost, it had gotten a little foggy out but not just up there where Clyde's shack sits; it was a little foggy all over this area. It sure don't happen all the time, but this here place does get some fog up in these parts and it's just as natural as early mornin' dew.

There have been some folks in the town claimed that they have seen ghosts floatin' around in the wisps of the fog we get sometimes. But the one that Clyde had seen that evenin' looked straight at 'im and he heard his name whispered out to 'im from that specter.

Come to think about it, those folks also claimed that they had heard voices callin' to 'em from them ghosts too.

When Clyde seen that specter and heard his name whispered out, he went straight into his shack and stayed inside with the door closed as he weren't about to experience another fright like he had when Jimmie disappeared that one day.

Oh, Clyde passed on some years later and no one really knows what had happened to Jennifer, but Elizabeth might know what happened to that woman 'cause she's Jennifer's daughter.

Sure don't believe you'll be gettin' any information from Elizabeth about her mother 'cause she damn sure won't say nothin' about it, but it sure is strange that she looks exactly like her mother and has her mother's ways too.

Ayuh, someone ought to take over old Clyde's place and fix it up some. Will that be you, maybe? Well, if you're here long enough, that is.

Thank you for listenin' to the story from the way I know it. I'm pretty sure you'll be comin' back here to this here mercantile tomorrow to learn more about this here township, and I'll be glad to pass on the story to ya.

I'm sure Frank will help ya out however he can while you're here in this place.

Take care and see you in the morrow.

SOULLESS RITES

Hello again. Today will be your fourth day with us here in Sacrificale Grove. Some of them young folks don't really last that long around here. Most end up in those woods north of here.

I can see you're holdin' your own, but I can also tell you're a little disturbed by this place.

Sure glad you met Frank and he was able to help ya out a little of what he could.

Pretty sure you're here to learn some more of the goings-on around here in the township and I'll tell you about them. There's somethin' that some of them womenfolk do that us regular folks call the Rites.

If you ask me, them women and those demented kids are soulless. Don't believe they have a soul in 'em.

But first let me tell ya that there's a little somethin' odd about the town itself. It's just a little thing really that most people who end up here don't really notice at all. Some of them folks do notice that there is somethin' missin' from here in Sacrificale Grove.

Yep, a few of them young folks point out that there's no church buildin' anywhere in the town. It's mostly them churchgoers that would notice that the church buildin' is missin'.

All them folks fail to notice that this here township has no graveyard, not even a family plot as old as this place is. I'm guessin' they figure that the cemetery is tucked away somewhere out of sight.

Some of them young folks speculate that the schoolhouse in the town may double as a worship center for the folks who live here in Sacrificale Grove. Well, that assumption just ain't really the case though.

Some of them womenfolk do gather somewhere at certain times of the year, with the exception of late spring, that is. Where they go, us regular folks don't really know.

Them women don the same style of dark robes, and at dusk they set out to wherever they meet until the first signs of dawn. Most of the time it's durin' the New Moon; when she is showin' her dark side is when them women head out. They sure do adhere to a different religion that doesn't require a buildin' to worship in from what I could tell.

As for the other folks in town, they're a little uneasy about them women's rituals and all. Some of them folks rather have that Holy book to tell 'em what to do and be up inside a worshippin' buildin' than to be outside.

Oh. There may have been a church at one time or another, but that was a long time ago. Nobody around here in this area knows how long ago that was. There weren't no church buildin' when old Thomas was alive and that was a long time ago. No one knows what had happened to that old church except for maybe those unnatural womenfolk. If you ask me, it could be that ruin Charley had stumbled upon when he was at that old haunt.

On the nights that them women gather together somewheres, there's a light blanket of fog coverin' the earth floor just a little over an ankle deep, and followin' those women out are them demented kids adorned in dark robes, which are tied with a sash. Wisps of fog swirls around the feet of those traversin' through that mist almost lookin' like specters of the night.

There were a few brave souls who ventured out to spy on them women and children to find out what they were up to. They were warned not to go but their curiosity got the better of 'em. Those people never came back on those nights. It's as if they went into those woods where that fog never lets up.

Them women go off into the forest that surrounds the town to do some kind of ritual of some sorts and it ain't the good kind neither. Well, they sure don't head out in the direction where this mercantile sits for some reason or another.

The other residents of the town start to hear some kind of faint chantin' as if it was comin' from everywhere but they can't understand what's bein' said at all 'cause it sounds like some kind of strange language them folks never heard of before.

Samantha may understand what the chantin' is all about, but she does her own rituals out of sight from the folks from town. Whatever magick is bein' conjured up, Samantha dispels it around her and the mercantile she now runs.

A few days after them women conduct their ritual, wherever they may have been, young travelers comes through that foggy barrier. Whether they stay around for a while or they end up goin' back the way they came was up to them.

Sometimes some of 'em ends up right back here sometime later.

Most of the time, majority of those people end up checkin' out this place. Then they end up goin' into those forbidden woods north of here if they haven't got spooked out first. Few of them young folks end up seekin' shelter in that old house up the road before they got to Jacobs Tavern.

There hasn't been a funeral for those who passed on like Clyde and Charley and others like them. There were never bodies to bury as their bodies turned into ash and dust not long after they had died. As always, one of them women would collect the ashes and dust that use to be a person in an urn of some type. They would leave with that urn, declarin' they know what to do with the remains. Those other folks in town don't know what them women do with the ashes of the dead and they dare not ask either. Don't believe them folks want to know what those death maidens do with it anyways.

Not too sure that's what happened to Clyde's ashes though. Nobody saw Clyde's remains in that shack of his when they got a peek up in there when a few folks from the town went to check in on 'im when no one had seen him in a few days. If one of them women came and collected his ashes, then he would have dropped dead somewhere outside of that shack 'cause they weren't able to get in with that charm bag buried underneath.

Some of the folks speculated that Clyde died of heart failure while out of his home and was never able to make it back in. Others thought he died peacefully in his sleep up in that shack of his and one of the women had someone go in and collect those ashes for 'em. You know how rumors get to be.

Either way, no one ever say his remains are outside or inside that shack.

Now Samantha got two of them urns sittin' on a mantle in Thomas Mercantile near the back end of the store. There was only one of those urns on the mantle when Charlene was runnin' the store. It wasn't long after Clyde was supposed to have passed away; Charlene was seen puttin' the other urn up on the mantle where it is now next to the first.

Patti had said that she swore she saw one of them women carryin' an urn when they went out of town to conduct their ritual, but she wasn't too sure about that. Those women could have been carryin' anythin' with 'em out on those nights.

Patti got that frightened look about her and didn't look like she slept too well with those bags under her eyes. She's awfully scared of them other women. She knew somethin' was wrong, not just with those other women, but the children as well when she ended up here in Sacrificale Grove. She has been livin' here for quite some time now.

Not long ago, Patti was just tendin' to her own business when she smelled a stink of somethin' rotten and decayed for a brief moment one day. She looked around about her to find out the source of that smell and caught sight of a walkin' dead that looked like it had been buried for quite some time. She looked at it for just a second then turned away real quick. Poor Patti was petrified after seein' that thing. She jumped a little when one of them women asked her if she was okay and if there was somethin' wrong.

Patti replied that she was fine and nothin' was wrong and quickly added that she had to go, and then she left to be around the other folks like her. She started stayin' in the guest house out back behind this here mercantile with me.

Patti, Frank and the other folks like us aren't really free of this place here. Whatever enchantment those women conjured up, curse more likely, it surrounds this area like a curtain, a foggy curtain. Folks here have no knowledge of the happenin's of the outside world anymore, except for when someone gets plucked from somewhere out on an old country road like you have been, then we get our news of the outside world.

Not many folks who live around these parts ever attempted to leave out either by the road or through the forest southbound or east. No one dared to attempt to travel north. Most don't seem to come back while others do, some days later that is, like Derrick Turner.

Derrick decided that he was gonna head out and try to see the outside world and try to get back to where he came from by followin' Hallow Creek south through the forest that way. Guess he figured it would be safest in the woods to the south with some concealment instead of on the road in plain view to where them women will know what he was up to.

Both Frank and Patti didn't think it was a good idea for Derrick to try to leave out as no one really knows what's out there and for Frank and Patti, they didn't want to know from what they experienced.

Well, it's a lot better than goin' through the woods up to the north and besides, those people who end up at this place had to have came from somewhere. That was Derrick's thoughts on it anyways, and Frank had to agree on that one as a lot of them young folks came from different places.

So Derrick set out and followed near the river south and the farther he went, the thicker the vegetation near the river gotten. He had to skirt around that vegetation and he sure did try to keep that river within eye sight but sure didn't do him any good though.

Derrick started to get into some foggy patches which started out just a thin blanket of mist on the forest floor the farther he went. That misty fog got thicker the deeper he went in, and he lost sight of that river 'cause of that fog and the foliage.

Derrick had thought about turnin' around and headin' back as he really didn't have anythin' to prove to anyone back in town. Nope, he didn't turn around and decided that he was gonna be determined to push right on through.

That misty fog got so thick that Derrick had to put his hands out in front of 'im to feel for some tree bark or some other obstacle that he might run into. He weren't able to hear the flow of Hallow Creek anymore at that point.

From what Derrick heard is that moss grew on the north side of the trees and there were plenty of trees with moss facin' him as he went southbound but by the time he got into that thick cloud of fog, there was no moss growin' on any of the trees or anythin' else for that matter, which kind of made 'im a little worried about the direction he was goin'.

Derrick trudged on for about an hour or so but couldn't really tell how much time went by up in there where he was, but he did know it was still daylight out but weren't able to see where the sun was at. When he had set out, the sun was on his left risin' from the east that mornin'.

Just when Derrick thought there was no end to that cursed fog, it started to thin out and he was able to see a little further out. When he finally emerged from that foggy mist, wisps of it covered the ground ankle deep. The sun was now on his right side appearin' to set in the western horizon.

When Derrick came out of that forest, he came upon the edge of an old dirt road that had been well used over the years. As he looked straight ahead to the other side of the road, he spotted what may have looked like an old buildin' set back in some woods which was bein' overtaken by vines and shrubbery and it was almost well hidden; he just about missed seein' it.

Derrick turned his head, looked off to his left and on down the road he saw some kind of sturdy structure on the opposite side of the road from 'im. It sure did seem awfully familiar in a lot of ways to him as he looked at the buildin' down the road.

Derrick turned his head to his right and eyed the side of a structure that looked just like Jacobs Tavern, and beyond the buildin' was a wooden bridge spannin' a river with that road goin' into a small town; if you want to call it a town that is.

Derrick just stood there for a while lookin' around at the familiar sights thinkin' to 'imself that this situation he was in wasn't right at all. He had known he couldn't have got turned around back in those woods, even though that fog was as thick as it was.

As he was ponderin' the impossibilities and probabilities, a voice broke into his thoughts, one that he recognized as belongin' to Frank. Well, apparently Frank was doin' some upkeep at the tavern when he noticed Derrick out by the roadside just standin' there lookin' around.

"Mr Turner? Is that you?" Frank had to ask that question as if in doubt that Derrick was really standin' there. It seemed that Frank hadn't seen Derrick for a long time.

Derrick did have a puzzled look about 'im wonderin' why Frank asked him that question in the way he did and commented on it and said he only been gone for almost a whole day and must have got turned around back there in the forest somewhere.

Frank stopped short on what Derrick just said and told Derrick that he had been gone for a couple of months, not the whole day.

Derrick couldn't believe what he just heard and Frank reaffirmed what he said and told Derrick that he should go on to Thomas Mercantile and get with some of the folks who had gathered there as the day just startin' out.

Derrick became a little puzzled by what Frank said about the day just startin' as it was supposed to be the end of the day as it was mornin' when Derrick set out and he still couldn't grasp the idea that he had been gone for a couple of months.

Well, Frank prodded the bewildered man on up to this here mercantile, then he went back to the tavern to continue his work before Derrick stepped out of the woods from the south.

As Derrick walked on towards Thomas Mercantile, he was thinkin' about how it could have been possible for him to be gone for two months when he'd only been out there in them woods for just a few hours of what it felt like to 'im.

Once Derrick got here to this here mercantile, Patti and I were taken aback 'cause we thought that he was gone forever and it surprised us that he was here at all. We did confirm what Frank told Derrick about 'im bein' gone for two months.

That's how it is for some folks who decided they wanted to leave out and escape from this place and get back to the world they came from. Most are never seen again while those few like Derrick comes back days later or maybe months, but it only felt like a few hours to 'em.

There have been a few outsiders who ended up in this here township and most of 'em ended up in that dead place in the woods just up north from here and disappeared.

Whatever kind of ritual magick those women do got this place in some sort of limbo and snatches up unsuspectin' young people as if they were to be sacrificed.

Most of us regular folks around here call it the Rites. It seems like them wicked ones don't want anyone leavin' out of this place. Those who do try to leave out and never return probably got stuck in that foggy barrier that surrounds this territory, just wanderin' around aimlessly. Couple of folks around here would like to believe that at least one person made it through to the outside world.

***

Some of the folks around here looks a little sickly like their energy is bein' drained or their blood, 'cause they have lost a little color in their face. Some of them womenfolk look more vibrant, and full of life, even though they have pale skin and they seem healthy as can be.

Them children seem to be full of life but if you look into their eye's, you could see somethin' evil and dead.

Seems like this place drains the life force out of some of the folks here and give it to them women and those kids. Perhaps it's those unnatural ones who are drainin' the essence out of the other folks. They really don't feel their energy drain out of 'em but they just mention that they're just a little tired, that's all.

When them folks get to Thomas Mercantile, they tend to be rejuvenated a little bit.

Guess that could be the reason why those who have passed away turn to dust and ash 'cause they were drained completely dry.

Those demonized kids don't seem to grow any older the longer you stay here. They may change their appearance ever so often but they stay the same age as always, and them kids been that young since I've been here and that's been about fifty years ago I should think.

Don't see how those women could have had any offspring when you really don't see a rounded tummy as if they're carryin' a child. Even when they were supposed to have given birth, you never see the child at all until they're grown, then they take over whatever their mother was doin'. Strange thing is that you never see the mother ever again.

Seems that them women always producin' a female, never a male, and their daughters always look just like 'em. You could swear they're their own mother.

All the original inhabitants of this place had died out except for them womenfolk and those children. If you ask me, them evil women never had any offspring of their own; they're just pretendin' to fool us folks.

Seems this place tends to replace those who have passed away by snatchin' those from the outside world. You can never know who is to be in service for them women or who is destined to end up in those woods up north. It just may depend on what type of ritual them women perform in honor of their gods.

Sometimes them strong-minded folks end up here from the outside world. Those are the kind of folks them women have a hard time gettin' to. Now that could be Samantha's doin' of gettin' them strong-minded folks here instead of them weak and timid ones.

Those strong-minded folks would notice somethin' wrong real quick like. It's not just the way the place feels to 'em but the lack of mirrors in any of the buildin's, even in the guest rooms at Jacobs Tavern.

It's said that mirrors reflect the soul of a person back to 'em. It could also be that mirrors reflect the true nature of a thing or creature that's bein' shown. Either way, when someone from far away brings a small mirror with 'em, it ends up bein' so shattered that they weren't able to see their reflection at all.

You might catch a reflection from a smooth surface of some standin' water before it gets disturbed or a highly polished item, that's if you can find one around this place that is, but you might see somethin' horrific or eerie in that reflection for just a second or two.

Them women like to keep the illusion in place as much as possible of the way some things may truly look like, especially themselves. It's a little harder to maintain that illusion with those strong-minded folks and them women don't like those kinds of folks no how. Neither do those little imps that are portrayed as children like them strong-minded folks.

Those vampiric women somehow know it's Samantha who has those types of folks come to this here place. Do believe it started with Rebecca, Samantha's grandmother, who started to get them strong-minded folks snatched up and bring 'em to this forsaken place.

There must have been some kind of fallin' out for Rebecca to break away from them other women like she did. Ayuh, there's some resentment between them women and Samantha now just like it was with Rebecca.

There may not be a mirror in the mercantile but Samantha keeps a basin filled with water at all times. She'll sternly tell ya that it's not for drinkin' nor for bathin' but for other purposes that you don't need to concern yourself with.

Well, that basin been there in the store since Rebecca put it in but it's now kept at the back end of the mercantile near Samantha's private quarters to keep folks from disturbin' it.

Well, that's it for today. If you feel up to it tomorrow and don't have a weak stomach, I'll tell ya about the seasons around here and what goes on durin' those times of the year. Some of it is very disturbin'.

If you're not too keen on goin' back to Jacobs Tavern, I'm pretty sure Patti will let you share her room for the night. It just might be a little safer and you might have better sleep than you have been these past couple of nights.

I'll see you in the morrow then, if you're still here that is.

SEASONS

I see that you're back with me this day. Take a seat and I'll tell ya about the seasons of this place and what takes place around here. I know that I have told you that time has no meanin' here but the seasons of the year seems to mark the passin' of time here, or so you might think that.

You're lucky enough to be brought here to Sacrificale Grove durin' the summer as opposed to what had happened not too long ago, but I'll get to that soon enough. It may be a bit disturbin' to sit through though to hear out this tale.

It won't be too long before autumn gets here and from the autumn equinox to Samhain, the area around here seem to start dyin' off. The leaves on the birch trees and the few oaks turn their color from the rich green hue to golden colors of yellow, red and orange, then finally brown which some of the leaves start to fall off and descend to the ground.

Every so often there is a shimmer durin' that time where you might see very old ruined buildin's throughout the township. It's almost as if the true nature of this place is tryin' to show itself.

That veil between the spiritual world and the mundane gets a little thinner the closer to Samhain, better known as Old Hallows Eve. You might see somethin' that probably wasn't there in the first place, but then again, you may never know.

Sometimes a light cloud of smoky fog blankets this whole area but not so thick to where you can't see durin' this time of the year.

You might catch a glimpse of some of those womenfolk lookin' like the dead walkin' or somethin' more vampiric for a brief moment when the shimmer passes through. That must have happened to Patti durin' that time period of the year when she saw what she saw. But there is that smell of death in the air when it happens around some of them womenfolk.

When there's a shimmer around one of those kids, you could swear that you may have seen the flesh on one side of their face gone which you will see ragged sharp teeth showin' and the canines longer than normal. Other times the lower portion of their face is transformed to where you will see sharp jagged teeth from one side of the face to the other with that hungry look in their eyes. In a split second afterwards, you will see that cute smilin' innocence as before but the eyes tell somethin' different.

On Samhain, that veil is thin enough to where you might see spirits in that swirlin' mist that hangs about this place at that time of year. You may see some things that really ain't there and might hear some growlin' and not know where it was comin' from. Out there in the misty fog that's swirlin' around the township and surroundin' dead woods, you may think that you saw some sort of beasts with mouths filled with sharp and jagged teeth, droolin' from their gapin' mauls and eyes that shines at night like a cat's.

The folks who have been here for quite a while have learned real quick to stay indoors at that time of the year and tried not to let them voices they hear disturb 'em too much. But if they need to get out takin' care of somethin', they try to go as a group of two or three.

Some weeks later, after the leaves have fallen completely and before the winter solstice, there will be a few inches of snow that will come down coverin' the ground. No winter wonderland this place will be.

When folks are brought here to Sacrificale Grove durin' that time, all they see around here are what looks like to them old ruined abandoned buildin's which they seem to be empty of life. That shouldn't fool you none 'cause there are folks somewhere's about.

Sometimes a few of them folks have to seek shelter in one of those rundown buildin's 'cause the weather took a turn for the worst with the wind pickin' up and the snow comin' down a little harder causin' snow drifts.

You might see one of them womenfolk out walkin' from one place to another just wearin' a simple gown in that frigid cold. On occasion they might look toward your way, other times they won't. On closer observation, you will notice that there is no indentation in the snow where the woman's feet had been, like she had no substance about her at all.

Sometimes one of the other folks in town will be out in that cold weather and you can tell that they got some substance about 'em 'cause they're havin' to trudge through that snow instead of float on top of it. The newcomers might think that those few who they see out might be the only ones in this ghost town but they're welcome to stay in what shelter they had found until the storm passes through. There ain't any help for those who took shelter in that old haunt just up the road from this mercantile.

Most of the time it's Frank out there on the cold snowy days that them outsiders see which he was instructed to tell them folks who came here, that there were no one else here and to have 'em believe that he was the only one in that town.

There has been a few times where a couple of the town folks bids the newcomers inside one of the buildin's, which they called home, for them young folks to get out of the cold frigid air and get warm. Those people might think that the townsfolks the only people in this rundown place after they had been wanderin' about for some time without seein' anyone.

Them townsfolks who brought in them young folks has to keep up the charade of bein' the only inhabitants of that town, but they don't like doin' it; it's what they were instructed to do.

Those young folks would hold up in one of the old buildin's for quite a spell whether they themselves sought out shelter or a couple of the townfolks invited 'em in from the cold. While inside tryin' to keep warm, one of 'em might hear a giggle of a child's laughter right outside when none of the others did. That one might see one of them kids out there in the cold if the person decides to take a peek out the window, then get it in their head that they wanna help that child and sneak off, gettin' separated from t'others.

There are other times when someone may have seen some sort of beast among the skeletal trees of the woods or somewhere far enough back to where they couldn't tell what manner of creature it was 'cause the snow been comin' down hard. Those folks might think it's either a large feline or canine at the size of a child or they might think they're seein' a creature that's a cross between a feline and canine.

Eventually them outsiders will disappear one by one over the course of their stay and end up in those woods just to the north where that misty fog sits. Except those few who just wouldn't fall for that type of shit and seem to be a little paranoid, and sense things really wrong about this place. That happens with most of the colored folks who ends up bein' drawn here.

It takes quite some time for them strong-minded folks to break and end up losin' their minds durin' that time of the year. Yep, it's a little harder to get at them strong-minded ones. It seems like them strong-minded folks may have more common sense than the others do. Ayuh, they sure do try to keep the group together as best as they could if there is a group of them young folks who end up here at the same time.

Those weak-minded ones tend to leave the group by themselves somehow without bein' noticed. That does seem to happen when there is a group of them young folks.

Don't you think that it's just the white folks who end up here; them colored folks and those who speak some other language also come to this township as well. Some of them white folks are easily fooled but those colored folks know somethin' ain't right the moment they get here. But still, somethin' happens to most of 'em. Old Clyde was one of them colored folks, one of the few who survived one of those winters.

Well, the winter season in this place is a real bitch for the folks who live here and for them young folks who end up here.

There is always a few bodies found frozen, and with the look on their faces, they may have died of fright. Sometimes you might find a partially eaten carcass up in those woods close by where that fog is. Yep, pretty gruesome way to go. There must be some sort of beast that comes out of that thick misty fog durin' the winter. There sure is no mercy for them folks who are brought here durin' that time of the year.

My advice is to stay indoors as much as possible 'cause there's always a terrible snow storm here. You'll sure will hear a lot of growlin' durin' that time, and ever so often there will be a howl comin' from everywhere. It may sound like there are several of large creatures out there in that storm.

The only safe place to be that I know of is right here at Thomas Mercantile. There must be some sort of force around this shop that keeps those things away from here, I'm guessin'.

Come springtime those beasts that were out terrorizin' the town apparently returns to wherever they may have came from and the snow begins to melt away. The strangest thing is, is that them kids are never seen durin' most of the winter months but if you do, their image fades away and you're left wonderin' if they were really out there, but when that snow melts and the days start to get warmer, you might catch one or two of them demented imps around Victoria when she's walkin' about.

As the vegetation start to show a little life and the grass gets a little greener, you might notice a smell out in the woods, just to the north of that dirt road that leads into town and out by Hallow Creek, as everythin' begins to thaw out. You won't notice that rotten smell while on the road itself or in the town; it's only if you go into them woods for anythin' that you smell somethin' like a rottin' corpse.

There has been a few folks who wandered in those woods and stumbled upon a rottin' body that looked like it's been eaten on by some large animal. That made them folks a little nervous about bein' out there in them woods; for one thing, they had no idea what kind of animal was out there that could have done such a thin', and another, them folks didn't know where that beast could be. No, they didn't stick around for too long, they got out of that area quick.

There's really no large animal out in those northern woods at all 'cause the animals around these parts apparently don't like to be up in the woods where that misty fog sits, except for maybe some crows. You might spot rabbits, squirrels, badgers, deer, or any other woodland critters in the woods on the south side of the main road.

The folks who have been livin' here in Sacrificale Grove for quite a while know that it was that beast or other monstrous creature that had came around durin' the winter.

Well, things seem to start to become normal for these folks who live here when the vernal equinox approaches. It may seem normal for us but for the folks just comin' here, nothin' is normal like they knew it to be for 'em.

Frank goes around fixin' some of the damage that was done durin' the winter season when the weather turns favorable near springtime. A lot of times you could find 'im in the old tool shop workin' or in the blacksmith shop workin' the old forge and poundin' away the workpiece on the anvil which he cools it down in the slack tub.

About a little over a month later, them women will have Frank and a couple of the other folks in town get things ready for a bonfire in the town common and have preparations for an upcomin' event. You might think it might be some sort of upcomin' celebration, but it ain't. It'll take a couple of days for Frank and those helpin' 'im to get things prepared for the ritual them women conducts.

Those folks in town dare not partake of the rituals them women would perform when that day comes. Some of the folks will leave out of town in the mornin' of the day of and head over here to Thomas Mercantile for that night. Them others would stay indoors and stay put and not peek out to see what would be goin' on, but there are those who are just a little too curious for their own good.

Some of us folks already know what would be goin' on the evenin' of that day. It has been goin' on every year, farther back than I been here.

Even Frank won't stay in town on that day. He comes out here to this mercantile and stays with Samantha and with some of the other folks from town.

Old Clyde, in his days, would spend the entire day here at the mercantile on the day of the ritual. He even spent the night here as well. It disturbed 'im greatly of what them women were doin' when they conducted their ritual in the town common. When he started stayin' at the shack he built for 'imself, Clyde was a little relieved that he didn't have to worry about what was goin' on in that town anymore.

The ritual that them women been doin' was witnessed by a few folks who were a little too curious for their own good. Some days later, after they had saw what they weren't suppose to see, they disappeared or were found dismembered by one of the other folks from town.

One of the folks who had seen what transpired on that night related his tale to another person while they were in Thomas Mercantile. Guess he thought he would have been safe here in the store to tell what he saw, but that wasn't the case for 'im. Rebecca, durin' her time, overheard what was said, and that ritual them women done was no shock to her at all.

Some days later, the person who had told the story disappeared and the one he told it to was found out by that old house on up the road. The body was torn in half and looked like it was partially eaten on and there were some crows feastin' on the body parts.

Charlene Roberta related this tale to me many years ago, informin' me that no harm would come upon me as long as I stay close to this mercantile, as I suggest that you should too as well, but never repeat it to anyone else in the town or anyone new who happens to come to this place.

Late in the afternoon on the day of the ritual, just like in the years precedin', one of the womenfolk would make sure those preparations were completed. In the recent years, it's been Victoria who made sure that things were ready for that evenin'.

When the sun started dippin' down in the western horizon, the pile of wood that had been stacked in the center of the common would burst into flames without anyone standin' close to it to get the fire goin'.

One of them women would be in a position what is known as a priestess and she would only be standin' just a couple of feet away from that wood pile when that fire started. Recently, Victoria been in that position of bein' the priestess.

She would have her face turned upward facin' the sky with her arms raised up above her head as if she was reachin' for the sky above. Then several robed figures would enter into the clearin' of the common from different directions like they were comin' out of the woodwork. There are twelve of them robed women who came out into the common circlin' the bonfire, and if you include the priestess, she'll make the thirteenth.

Smaller figures the size of the children came into the common as well and went to the priestess and stood behind her a ways.

Two of them women were seen carryin' a long wooden pole that's about roughly nine feet in length with a linen-wrapped person tied to it. It could have been a man or woman who was blanked and wrapped in that linen and tied up to that pole.

Those women stood that pole up on one end and it sunk into the hard ground with ease between the priestess and those little ones. It seemed like it didn't matter if that person who was tied to the pole was upside down or not.

After placin' the wooden pole, them robed women took their respective places around that roarin' fire, and after they all had gathered around the fire pit, the sun had just dipped below the western horizon and the rays of the sunlight were fadin' with the stars startin' to twinkle in the cloudless night sky overhead.

From what it had looked like was that the person that's been tied to that pole was movin' a little, or it could have been a trick in the mind of those few who had witnessed the ritual over the years that was caused by the glow of the flickerin' flames dancin' around on it.

All of a sudden, a woman's voice spoke out but it was in some sort of language that none of the folks who were still in the town that night could understand what was bein' said. Those folks have never heard that strange language before and it was more like chantin' the longer they heard it. Shortly after, the other women's voices joined the first bein' in unison with each other.

After those women had been chantin' for a while, they started to get louder and louder until it was almost unbearable to the folks who had stayed back in the town. Those who were stayin' here at the mercantile heard a faint echo of that chant back in town. Then the chantin' stopped and what followed was silence.

From what was observed by those few folks who had watched the ritual was that those women took off their dark robes and just let the garment fall to the ground at their feet. Even the priestess discarded her robe and those women were standin' around that fire completely nude, but them others who were standin' behind the priestess and the person tied to the pole stayed clothed the entire time the ritual was conducted.

Those women then started to sway back and forth as if they were swayin' to the sound of some music that only they could hear. It also looked like they were in rhythm with the flames that was dancin' up out of that wood pile to the sky.

They then started to dance around the bonfire counter-clockwise and their chantin' began again. At first, they danced slowly around while chantin' their chorus then slowly began to pick up their pace until they were dancin' in a frenzy.

As them women were dancin' in that frenzied state and doin' their chant, the fire changed hues from an orange-red glow to a greenish color, which was eerie for them folks who were watchin' and for them who only saw that green light faintly comin' through the windows.

The facial expressions of them women began to change soon after and their faces weren't normal-lookin' anymore. They looked more vampiric and beastly while they were dancin' in frenzy around that fire in the common and their naked bodies began to be decayed and rottin'.

The person who been bound to that wooden pole stickin' out of the ground was movin' and squirmin' at that point all the while the chantin' was still goin' on but not in a sweet womanly voice but more guttural and hideous in that strange hypnotic language.

One of them monstrosities had stopped its frenzied dancin' in front of that wooden pole with the tied-up blanketed person. It stood there facin' the soon-to-be sacrifice and as it did, very large bat wings sprouted from the thing's back, spreadin' out. The others soon stopped their dancin' and their chant had also ended, and slowly converged on the linen-wrapped figure who was strugglin' to get loose but to no avail.

Those thirteen monsters then tore into that doomed individual like savage beasts, rippin' the garment away, tearin' into the flesh, and the other residents of the township that chose to stay in their homes there had heard an inhuman scream of agony.

Even though those townsfolks knew that it was a person screamin', they didn't know who it was, but they figured it was someone who had ended up in this place unaware of what would happen to 'em.

After a short while, the scream those townsfolks heard had died to a gurgle, then silence as those demonic beasts continued to ravage the body, which was now on the ground as the rope was cut by their claws. After them creatures had devoured most of the body, the one which the leathery wings had sprouted from its back tossed what was left into the midst of them robed imps that had gathered behind the carnage.

Those few folks who were a little too curious by watchin' what was happenin', they saw those little tykes quickly tear into what was left like a pack of animals, which those things are the creepy children that are seen at the school house or with Victoria at times.

While them short robed beasts were eatin' on the rest of the carcass and crunchin' on the bones, the nude vampire-like creatures started to dance around that greenish bonfire as if they were eloquent marionettes. As they were dancin' around that green flame, their faces and bodies began to change back to what they had normally looked like before, with blood coverin' their mouths and runnin' down their necks and bosoms.

Them women took their respective spots around the fire after they had danced for a while and began to chant again in that strange language. That greenish flame turned back to the reddish-orange hue all the while they were chantin' in that musical voice of theirs.

After they had been chantin' for a while, their voices died down to nothin' and they all gathered their garments off the ground and loosely donned the robes over their bodies.

In the meantime, those little beasts had finished off that carcass, bones and all, and all that was left was blood on the ground where it once was along with the pieces of the linen it was shrouded in.

Then them women left out from the common as the little ones gathered around the priestess as she was headin' out, and that fire that was blazin' died away to nothin', which left the place in darkness.

The next day the common was found empty of any evidence that anythin' ever happened the night before. That wooden pole was gone along with any bits of linen that the person was wrapped in, and even the blood from the victim was missin' along with the burnt wood that was used for the bonfire. It was as if nothin' had ever happened that night.

Us folks here in Sacrificale Grove have noticed that the vegetation surroundin' this here township was in full bloom as opposed to what it had looked like before when the birch trees and other plants were just buddin'. That event happens once a year on that night late in the spring some time before summer hits.

It may seem like them women don't care if anyone watches on that night but you'll be wrong about that. Other times of the year, they go off somewhere secluded for some reason other than what I have told ya before.

In the summer months this place is a little calmer although them young folks still end up in this place on occasion. Very few of them folks ever get to stay alive and stay here as long as I have and some of the others in town. Guess them creatures masqueradin' as humans keep a few of us folks alive to make this place seem a little normal for them folks who are drawn into this township, but them folks comin' here soon find out that this place ain't natural at all.

Yep, this place here is somewhat quiet of most of that supernatural shit most of the summer, and when it comes to a close and autumn begins, the cycle will soon start all over again.

For the folks here in this township, they get themselves prepared for the upcomin' events mentally and try to strengthen their resolve so they don't go insane when autumn comes about. Unfortunately, a few of 'em aren't able to take it anymore and they end up goin' mad or they just disappear altogether with no trace of their existence.

Some of the other folks, like myself, have a strong mind about 'em and a strong will.

Well, Samantha does help out most of the folks here as well. She has her own way of doin' things, but the way she does 'em, you might think she's just like them other women. In a way she just might be like 'em, but she does her rituals to benefit the poor souls who have to deal with the evilness of those monsters and the children.

This is what' it's like around this area and been goin' on way before I was brought here. Us regular folks do age here but it's probably due to our energy bein' drained or our essence sucked out. But for some reason bein' around this here mercantile, the process is slowed down some.

You probably have taken a little tour of the township I'm guessin'. You must be wonderin' why you haven't seen any official in town, or not even a constable or maybe a deputy to take care of the vagrancy around here.

If you come back tomorrow, I'll tell ya more about that, but for now this old man needs some rest.

THE CONSTABLE

Well, hello, how are you doin' this fine day? Good I hope. Take a seat as I'm guessin' that you've probably noticed that there ain't no constable here in Sacrificale Grove, or any other kind of town official for that matter. There's a constable's office close to the town hall with a jailhouse right in between just to the east of the town common.

Both the jailhouse and the constable's office are in such disrepair, they're about to collapse on themselves. The town hall is in pretty good shape; that's 'cause Frank has done some repair work on it on occasion.

Some of the townsfolks gather at the town hall sometimes to hold a meetin' there. I don't go there anymore, but Frank does sometimes.

There ain't been a constable here in this township since before I came. No one knows what happened to the constables or why this town ain't got one anymore. It may have somethin' to do with those women takin' charge of this place.

About the only area they have no control of is Thomas Mercantile and Clyde's shack. It appears that this here store is well protected from those demonized women who have control of the town itself and most of the area surroundin' it.

That town hall is the exception though. Those women don't really bother the folks when they hold their meetin's up in there. Guess them women like to have the folks think they got some say about how the town is run, but I know better than that.

Do believe that Frank knows who really runs the town. He ain't all that stupid or timid-minded if you ask me. He plays at it though to keep most of the folks fooled of how he really is, especially them women, but those women knows more than what they're lettin' on. But he does try to look after some of the folks, even the ones who are new to this place.

Yep, Frank sometimes attends the meetin's just to find out what them folks are talkin' about, but he stays in the back and don't engage in the discussions.

Those folks are always talkin' about stuff they have talked about on many occasions. They keep sayin' that there has got to be somethin' done about the situation that they're in and about them women and demonized kids, but they're too afraid to do anythin' about it. They might be hopin' that someone would come along and take care of things for 'em.

That town hall ain't too close to the school house of which the folks in town are glad of that.

There's a few of the regular folks who don't attend the meetin's. Guess to them it's just a waste of time and nothin' is really done. There's very few of them folks who believe that they're in some sort of leadership position. Just because some of 'em been here in this township longer than some of t'others don't make 'em leaders or town officials.

If they think they're in some type of leadership position, they're bullshittin'; they ain't in charge of shit. I know who really runs this place and so does Frank and Patti.

Victoria doesn't seem to like the idea of the 'townfolks havin' their meetin's in the town hall. You can see her standin' somewhere some distance away just starin' at that buildin' while those folks are in there. Sometimes those kids are with her, gathered around her like a pack of animals surroundin' their leader, starin' at the town hall. Somethin' ain't natural the way that woman and them kids just standin' there watchin' them folks go into the buildin' and stayin' there until they come out when their meetin' is over.

Well, Victoria really don't do anythin' about them folks havin' their meetin's 'cause Elizabeth allows the folks to have their get together. Elizabeth seems to be more of a motherly type but don't let that fool ya. Just like her mother, Jennifer, Elizabeth does have her way with some people. If you remember what happened to Jimmie, you know what I'm talkin' about. Do believe Elizabeth is Jennifer as she looks just like her and has her ways, but she denies that claim and insists that Jennifer was her mother.

Before Frank got here to this township, nobody really done any work on that town hall or did much maintenance on the other buildin's in town. It was his idea to fix up the town hall so the folks could meet there instead of meetin' in a small cramped room of someone's home.

Frank just saw a lot of things that needed repair when he ended up in this place, so he took it upon 'imself to start fixin' up some of the buildin's and doin' other maintenance that was bein' neglected. Guess that's why them women kept 'im around for so long, but they wouldn't let 'im fix up the jailhouse or the constable's office though.

It's like them women make up the laws around here and sometimes enforces 'em, but it's them women who are bein' lawless and t'other folks has to police themselves. Most of the folks in this township believe there should be some kind of law official, but they sure don't do nothin' about it for fear of repercussion.

Some of the young folks who are drawn here in Sacrificale Grove don't understand why there ain't no sheriff in the town to deal with some of the problems that's goin' on in the area that they are witnessin' or havin' to deal with themselves. But there are a few of 'em who figure out real quick that it has somethin' to do with the unnatural way this place feels and how some of the women are, like the ones they end up meetin', like Elizabeth, or the ones who greets 'em warmly, like Susan Moore. Them young folks also find out how unnatural those kids are as well, of which them kind of folks are the strong-minded ones who end up in this township.

There were a few times that I know of where someone had tried to bring order to this place and implement some laws to the lawlessness and that was met with dire consequences and those people ain't around anymore. I don't know how many times that had happened before I was brought here.

I remember one such fella not too long ago and he came here just like everybody else except them pasty women and those fiendish children. Samantha has also been here her whole life as well.

The lad noticed a lot of things that are off here in Sacrificale Grove and he did seem to have a strong mind about 'im, but thinkin' back on it, it may have been just a show he was puttin' on. Believe he was a lawman wherever he was brought from, or at least that's what he told some of the folks in town. He damn sure wasn't a true constable, but more like a deputy if he was a lawman.

The young man's name was Rowland. To me he seemed to be like a little cocky bastard. He was brought here well before Derrick decided to try to leave out from this place.

Rowland had asked where the sheriff was at when he saw some things wrong, just like when he saw them kids outside of that schoolhouse not doin' nothin' but lookin' at 'im. He mentioned that they ought to be in school and not botherin' anybody, then inquired about where their parents were when they was messin' with the other folks who had come to this place.

He sure did get frustrated when he was bein' givin' the runaround about where the sheriff was at when he asked about it and couldn't understand why them women always kept sayin' constable even when he said sheriff. He got so fed up that he took it upon 'imself to look for the constable's office on 'is own.

I don't believe he was all that strong-minded, but he sure was stubborn as hell. Well, some of them women tried to get at 'im in his head, but he was so full of 'imself that he didn't take the bait. Like I said, he was a little cocky bastard.

Some of t'other folks tried to tell 'im that there weren't no sheriff here in this township, but he just didn't listen.

After a while he found that old ruin that was the constable's office after searchin' for quite a bit, and he seemed to be a bit confused and couldn't believe that the old rundown place was the sheriff's office and the old buildin' next to it was the jailhouse.

Rowland noticed Frank nearby doin' some work and strolled up to 'im and asked about where exactly the sheriff's office was located at, and Frank pointed out the rundown structure to the young man. As Rowland was walkin' off, Frank overheard 'im sayin' somethin' about things was gonna change around here. Guess the fella was sayin' it to 'imself but not very quietly.

Then he stopped in his tracks, turned around and asked Frank where the folks in this here backwoods of a town go to hold their meetin's. Frank pointed out the town hall he had renovated and then tried to warn Rowland about the strange things goin' on in this place and those creatures masqueradin' as women and them queer kids, but Rowland cut 'im off and told 'im to gather the folks for an emergency town meetin'.

Then that cocky some bitch turnt back around and walked off leavin' Frank stumped.

Reluctantly Frank went off and fetched all the folks he could and when he did, he noticed Victoria standin' off in the distance starin' in the direction where Rowland walked to. Frank scurried away as quickly as he could and be done with informin' the townfolks of the meetin'. Well, he never did attend that meetin' and neither did I.

There were some folks who went just to hear 'im out; t'others weren't about to hear no bullshit from someone who don't know jack shit about what's happenin' here in this township.

Rowland had told those who attended that since there weren't no sheriff or even any deputies nowhere in town, he was gonna take up the position of bein' sheriff of the township and things were gonna change under 'im, and the vagrants were gonna be taken care of. Then he demanded that the first thing on the agenda was to get that jailhouse and sheriff's office built back up, and in the meantime, he was gonna use that town hall as his office.

He then told them folks that he wanted cooperation from 'em and said he was gonna demand it from most of the wretched women and tried to ease their minds about him straightenin' things out around here. I don't think none of them folks in that meetin' ever bought into that bullshit he was spewin' forth.

He also mentioned somethin' about bein' respected of which it sounded more like he was demandin' it and all the folks in town needed to respect the laws that he was gonna implement.

Now that was just his second day here in Sacrificale Grove when he held that meetin' in the town hall. The first day Rowland ended up here from the world he was from, he seemed a bit arrogant about a lot of things here in this township.

Upon enterin' Thomas Mercantile, he mentioned that the place needed to be shut down after lookin' around for a brief moment and also said somethin' about that it was a wonder that the health inspectors, whatever that is, hadn't condemned the store.

Rowland asked Samantha the whereabouts he was, at which she replied that he was in the township of Sacrificale Grove, which he didn't really believe that 'cause he had never even heard of this place at all.

He then had asked her if she had a business license, whatever that may be, to run this here store. Well, he left out the mercantile in disdain and proceeded up the dirt road towards the town itself.

He passed Jacobs Tavern without a second glance and went over the bridge spannin' Hallow Creek, and as he strolled into the town he looked around observin' some of the buildin's and seein' if he could spot anybody out and about.

He walked past the blacksmith shop as well as the tool shop, which was on his left and what looked like a couple of old houses on his right. As he passed the stables, there was what looked like some sort of a business-type of buildin' off to his right, which is not in operation anymore these days.

When Rowland got closer to Damnosus Gifts, he saw Susan Moore standin' in the doorway of the store, which faced the town common. He did notice the schoolhouse towards the eastern edge of the common, which none of the kids were out there in school yard at that time.

Susan greeted the young man in a flirtatious way, which he was kind of put off by, and then he was invited into her store. Rowland was a little apprehensive at first but reluctantly went in as he thought that the buildin' wasn't really fit to be workin' in.

When he entered the shop, there' was a pigment smell he didn't care for at all and looked about the interior at a glance and what he saw made 'im wonder if anythin' in that store was legal.

Susan offered Rowland a gift of his choosin', and we both know what that supposed 'gift' is, just to welcome 'im to the little town, but apparently his thinkin' was that she was tryin' to bribe 'im and he sure said as much to her. He also said that the authorities needed to shut her little operation she got goin' down.

He left out of that store mutterin' about not wantin' nothin' to do with what that woman got goin' on in that shop of hers and to try to find somebody who's with the authorities. What he didn't understand was that there are no authorities here in Sacrificale Grove and haven't been for longer than I been here.

As soon as Rowland left out of the buildin', the seductive smile Susan was portrayin' was gone and the evilness in her eye's surfaced, and bein' on the outside of Damnosus Gifts, he saw them children out in the courtyard of the schoolhouse and he just assumed that they were out on a recess break while Victoria was standin' on the porch of the school.

It did seem a little odd to 'im that the little devils were just standin' in a group lookin' in his general direction instead of playin' like normal kids do, and he may have been wonderin' if Victoria was wearin' an eighteenth-century-style dress, but he dismissed that thought quickly and proceeded to find someone else worth talkin' to in that town.

Well, he did think that the town itself was abandoned at first when he didn't see anybody before comin' across Susan, then he figured there had to be some others besides those women and kids he saw and one old man sittin' on the porch of Thomas Mercantile. He never did bother to ask me anythin' that needed to be knowin', guess he knew more than I did, that condescendin' prick.

I guess he just strolled around town some, takin' a peek in some of the buildin's, as he was seen walkin' around to find any other person to get some information.

As he was headin' back to where he started, he spotted a few folks enterin' into Jacobs Tavern in the distance from where he was. He then decided to go on back across the bridge and go inside the old tavern and upon enterin', he met up with a few other young folks who were also drawn here talkin' to Elizabeth.

She had given those folks a warm greetin' when they came into the place and offered 'em a room for the night when Rowland entered.

Bein' a want-a-be constable pretendin' to have that air of authority, Rowland asked the newcomers who they were and why they were here in this township as if he was interrogatin' 'em and actin' like he was runnin' this here township.

Elizabeth spoke up before anybody else could voice any questions and calmly told Rowland that those folks were just guests in her establishment.

Then one of the guy's in the group told the want-a-be that they didn't really know how they had gotten where they are now and they had to pass through some unusual thick fog on foot and didn't even know that this here town even existed.

One of the young women, bein' colored, hadn't felt right the moment she came to this place and everythin' about it was wrong to her. The moment Rowland went into the tavern, she sensed that he had disdain toward her for some reason, but for the other young folks she came with he seemed a little more lenient towards.

Elizabeth sure did see through his façade and reminded Rowland that they were guests and there would be no trouble started in her establishment; she then asked 'im if he too would like a room as well.

Somehow Rowland's hard exterior softened a bit and he complied with Elizabeth's wishes, and he ended up gettin' a room for that night of which I believe Elizabeth had gotten into his head.

At a later time, Rowland did ask them folks if they had met a deputy or the sheriff of the town when they had gotten to this here place and they replied that they hadn't yet.

Do believe his first night here was worst for 'im than the other folks who spent the night at Jacobs Tavern 'cause he had a haunted look in his eyes on his second day in this place, but he played it off like nothin' was botherin' 'im. I'm guessin' that's why he started stayin' in the town hall while he was stayin' in this township afterwards.

Rowland kept gettin' on Frank about fixin' up that jailhouse and constable's office and Frank kept sayin' that he would, but he never did 'cause of them women. Rowland also kept givin' some of the townfolks and those newcomers a hard time on occasion bein' that he had gotten it in 'is head that he was a man of authority just 'cause he had made 'imself sheriff of Sacrificale Grove.

Some of the older folks in town had tried to warn 'im of what really happens here in this township but he just didn't listen to 'em and brushed it off like he didn't really care.

There were many times that Rowland had tried to shut down Susan's shop 'cause he believed that she was dealin' in some sort of shady activities, but each time Victoria had 'im go off and investigate somethin' else like vandalism or a body had turnt up in the woods on the north side of the main dirt road, partially eaten or some other death that had occurred. Guess she let 'im play at bein' constable for a while, while she was playin' 'im like a cat does a mouse before that cat devours the mouse.

Oh, Rowland was also busy with some of the young folks goin' missin' not long after they had gotten here.

Each day of his stay here in this township them little tykes gave 'im the creeps and he always wondered why there ain't no social services, like there's any here in this place, to take charge of those little brats, as he calls 'em.

Patti had told Rowland off one day sayin' that he had no idea what he was gettin' 'imself into and she did not want nothin' to do with 'im and that he had best leave her alone and just stay away 'cause she didn't want to be a part of what he was doin'.

All this shenanigan with Rowland took place durin' the spring of last year.

Rowland sure did like to talk up a big game like gettin' the Feds involved to take care of what was happenin' around here if only he was able to find a way to get word out.

Whenever new folks end up here, Rowland also likes to get into their business, like why they were here, what business they had for bein' here, and probably to see if those folks were troublemakers just because they were young. But when some of 'em disappeared, he just assumed that most of 'em left town to go somewhere else not knowin' that them folks ended up in those woods up north from here. He still had to deal with some of the deaths that had happened with some of the other folks who had come here.

There were a couple of young folks who ended up goin' mad just before they died while Rowland was still here. Apparently those two spent the night in that old haunt just up the road from this mercantile. Don't really know how they found that house, mayhap they were led there somehow.

I do believe now that those monstrous women had plans for that little prick.

Us older folks who been here in this place for quite a while knew the signs that the yearly ritual them women perform in town was comin' very soon. When preparations were goin' on,

Rowland may have either been tryin' to stop what was happenin' or was tryin' to find out what kind of festival that was planned. He sure found out soon enough.

Just like always, most folks came here to Thomas Mercantile while t'others stayed in the homes they had claimed.

The day before the ritual, no one ever saw Rowland at all anywhere in the town or the surroundin' area. No one seen 'im the day of or any of the days there after anymore either.

Some of us folks may know what had happened to Rowland, but none of us ever talks about it ever. That is just no way for a person to go out, even if they may be a prick at times.

That young colored woman is still here. Like I said, the moment she got here, she knew things weren't right with this place.

She sure did keep her distance from them women and creepy kids and also tried to avoid Rowland as much as possible while he was here. She tends to stay here at this here mercantile as much as she can.

That town hall may have doubled as a courthouse way back in the day when this township was founded. The thing is there ain't no judge here either.

Even though there ain't no constable or any other town official, the ones who really run this place are them vampiric women who change their identities after so many years.

Well, that's all I can tell ya for now. If you're gonna wander around, do be careful and not stray too far from this mercantile.

If you're incline to give an old man company, I do appreciate that, if you're willin' to sit a spell. I just might have another story to tell sometime at a later date, but who knows, until then be safe and take care.

THE MANSION

I'm glad you came back to join me on this porch. It's been a few days since I last talked to ya. I see that Samantha has given you somethin' for protection since I told ya about that ritual that happens near the end of spring.

I'm guessin' you want to know a little more about this here township of Sacrificale Grove. From your exploration you probably know that there's a mansion on the eastern edge of town that could have been the mayor's house at one time or another. The place is surrounded by a wrought iron fence with a wide openin' towards the front of the mansion. That entrance is wide enough for a horse and buggy to go through, mayhap two at the same time.

The courtyard is thick with grass and weeds and a few oak trees where a couple of 'em looks dead and leafless as t'others look like they're about to die off.

The pathway to the front entrance of the old place is an old cobblestone roadway which the vegetation is growin' between the rocks of the path.

That old buildin' is a large three-story structure built from stonework and timber, almost havin' a castle-like appearance. That old structure was built on top of a small hummock which overlooks the town. It may have been built to last but there are parts of that mansion that look like it's about to crumble down. Most of the window panes are either broken in places or gone. It sure is much bigger than that house just on up the road from this mercantile.

The main entrance is a double set of large doors made out of oak. There are times where those doors are closed and other times one of 'em is partially opened. Every so often you might see one of them women standin' in the doorway of that mansion. There are times where you might have thought you seen someone lookin' out one of the windows and when you take a second look, there ain't anyone there.

That place does have an ominous feel to it. It's almost as if it was lookin' down on ya. Ain't nothin' about that place is natural. A lot of the townfolks don't like to go near that buildin' and most don't even like to look at it at all.

It seems to have a dark evil presence about it. It may have to do with those women taken up residency in that old mansion. They are often seen comin' and goin' from that place.

One of the women who is always standin' in the doorway of the main entrance goes by the name Ann Price. She always seems to have a sweet friendly smile displayin'. You would think that she's a real decent person to be around, but you'd be dead wrong.

She is friendly with a lot of people, even the young folks who are drawn into this township. You wouldn't think she's with them other women but she definitely is.

Ann has made it look like she was also drawn into this place just like t'others as well. She played her part so well that I even believed it. She wasn't known as Ann Price when I came here so many years ago; she went by a different name back then.

She would also freak out about how creepy them children are when she's with those who just came here. She points out how those kids are always standin' around in a group together starin' at the newcomers and even at some of the folks who had been here for many years.

When those little heathens start messin' with them young folks who are new to this place, Ann voices her fear of 'em and don't wanna chase after those little creatures, but she does get into them folk's heads, about one or two of 'em, to go and run after them kids. Eventually those young folks end up goin' up into those woods where that misty fog sits or where that old house is just up the road. There's a few times where she saves very few of them folks from that demise.

Ann had mentioned somethin' about that schoolhouse where those kids are congregated at most of the time. Some of them other folks wonder about that buildin' as well but she then directs their attention to that novelty shop that Susan runs.

Sometimes she'll see Susan first, other times the person who's with her will see that woman, then Ann will get them folks to check out that store of which she will lead 'em in there so they can be persuaded into pickin' one of the cursed charms. None of them folks will ever see her get one as it was just a ruse to get them folks into that shady shop.

Ann doesn't act out the part of someone who was drawn into this township like t'others all the time. You'll see her at that mansion at times but not just standin' in the doorway but wanderin' the courtyard. Her appearance would be more like that of an ethereal spirit floatin' about.

Do believe that figure that some folks have seen lookin' out the windows of that mansion could have been Ann, but don't take my word for it.

You can see that large structure on top the hummock from the town hall. Most of the townsfolks who go to the town hall and have their meetin's there tries to ignore that castle-like structure as it's dark and forbiddin'.

That mansion is some distance away from the town hall but those folks can still feel its presence loomin' over 'em, so when they conduct their meetin's it's quick and to the point 'cause them folks don't really wanna stay too long there.

There has been a few times where Ann has led some of them young folks into that mansion for them to check it out. A lot of 'em has never come back out after enterin' that place. A few did come out runnin' scared shitless, and not just out the front entrance but out the back and into the woods behind that evil place.

Most of 'em was too frightened to talk about what happened while they were in there, but there were a few who did, while stumblin' over their words and stutterin' some.

Frank was almost led into that damned buildin' but Elizabeth stopped Ann from takin' him in there 'cause he had done a little minor work on Jacobs Tavern when he first went in to seek shelter on his first night here. He then worked on Susan's store for her when he seen somethin' that needed fixed.

He told those two women that he liked workin' with his hands and loved bein' able to see the potential in different objects and also expressed his interest in workin' with wood and doin' carpentry and was adapt on doin' maintenance on wooden structures at his young age.

So Elizabeth saw a need for such a person here in Sacrificale Grove as no one else in the town wanted to do anythin' about keepin' the place functional; therefore Ann never did try to get Frank to go in that place of horror again for the reason she does others.

It wasn't long after Frank had been here for a while doin' some repairs to a few of the buildin's when Elizabeth had inquired 'im about doin' some work on the old mansion.

Upon seein' that old stone structure, Frank had second thoughts about goin' up to that place. It sure did creep 'im out as much as those kids did, but Elizabeth reassured 'im that he would be fine and nothin' would happen to 'im.

He told her that he had to think about it before decidin' on whether or not he would fix it up some for her.

From what Frank was findin' out about this township the longer he stayed here, his doubts about goin' to that gothic horror grew stronger by the day.

I do think that Elizabeth had gotten Ann to be in good terms with Frank 'cause of her good nature towards others up to a certain extent. Don't let that good nature of hers fool ya 'cause it's just a farce.

Ann had been seen around Frank talkin' to 'im and, as always, she displayed her sweet smile toward 'im, proddin' 'im about goin' up to the mansion. She reinforced what Elizabeth had told Frank about him bein' safe and nothin' bad would happen to 'im. She may have let somethin' slip about him bein' important to them women, and he was to be kept alive to make sure the town looked good and not too rundown when newcomers are brought here.

After several weeks of havin' Ann keepin' Frank company while he did some minor work, he reluctantly agreed to do some repairs to the castle-like structure, even after she had told 'im that she would be with 'im while he was up inside that place. She even told 'im that he wouldn't be goin' up there durin' the night but she would make sure it was a bright sunny day.

When that day came, Frank just stood a ways from that gothic horror lookin' at it with dread. As he was lookin' up at it, one of them women came out and stood at the entrance and eyed Frank hungrily, but apparently there was an unspoken communication between Ann and the other woman, 'cause Frank is still here well and alive.

Ann then took Frank's hand in hers and proceeded up the slope to the old place, which he seemed to be a bit nervous about goin' up there, so he took 'is time gettin' to the front door with Ann leadin' 'im as t'other woman watched 'em make the trek to her.

When Frank was introduced to t'other woman, she called herself Carrie Wilkes and she told 'im that she knew about 'im 'cause she had already seen 'im around town doin' various odd jobs fixin' up the township.

Ann informed the redhead that Frank was there to do some repair work that needed to be done, and with that them two women ushered 'im in.

The interior was in shambles: cobwebs on the banister of the staircase and in the corners of the many rooms, a layer of thick dust coverin' everythin' (which is weird, 'cause them women are roamin' in that place a lot, but a few places where someone may have been), boards loose or off from the walls and floors, the candelabra loosely hangin' from the ceilin', which looked like it could fall at any moment, and the floorin' creaked with protest as he walked around (which he did say at one time that it was strange 'cause the two women were with 'im as well but the floors creaked with only his weight, not theirs).

Well, the whole time Frank was in there, Ann and Carrie stayed with 'im and there were many rooms and places in that buildin' they did not allow 'im to go for some reason or another. He did find it a little odd that when he tried to assess the damage in certain areas, those two women detoured 'im somewhere else like they didn't want 'im to see certain things in there.

After his somewhat little tour of the place, Ann led Frank out with Carrie followin' closely behind, and when Frank and Ann was outside, Carrie bid him farewell and said that she hoped to see 'im again soon, and the fiery redhead slithered back into the premise.

Frank did give a sigh of relief when he was walkin' away from that buildin' as the whole time he had been in there he felt his heart tryin' to thump out of 'is chest as he was too terrified of bein' in the devil's den.

Well, Ann did reiterate to 'im that nothin' was gonna happen to 'im as they were walkin' down the path and pointed out that he did live through the ordeal of bein' in the place with her bein' by his side protectin' 'im, which Frank had to agree with that.

Sometime later Elizabeth approached Frank to see if he would actually do some repairs to the mansion and he told her that he would as long as Ann was there with 'im to make sure t'others wouldn't do anythin' to 'im as apparently he grew fond of that girl even though he knew what she really was. So an agreement was struck and he spent a few days workin' on that place.

He did see a few of t'other women, which out of the corner of his eye's he noticed that Ann gave a look to 'em as if she was in some sort of silent communication with 'em, tellin' them to leave 'im alone.

Frank did as much as he could and even though he was up in there durin' the daytime, that place was startin' to get to 'im.

I believe it was Victoria who made the decision for Frank to end the repairs he was makin'. Well, he did see her with Ann talkin' to her in hushed tones and afterwards Ann told Frank that what he had done was good enough and he didn't have to come back anymore. He sure was relieved to hear that he didn't have to go back to that dark shadowy structure anymore. You can still see Ann with her chirpiness alongside Frank on occasion but she mostly went back to what she had been doin' before she talked Frank into goin' into the mansion. She never did try to get 'im to go up to that place afterwards, but she does get some of t'other young folks up in there who end up in this township whenever she feels a little frisky.

Even though the place has a forebodin' presence and some of them folks don't really want to go up there, Ann does have a way to get those young folks to go in that old structure. Very few folks decide to go up to that house of horrors themselves when none of them women even tempt 'em. Some go just out of curiosity and others do it from a dare. Most of those young folks never came back out while those few who did ran out of that place stumblin' over their own feet. You may see one of them women come out those doors with a smirk on her face lookin' at them folks runnin' for their lives. Sometimes it's Carrie with her fiery red hair or Ann with her ethereal form or one of t'others except for Veronica and Elizabeth. Them two are pretty much no-nonsense types even though Elizabeth may be the motherly type.

***

If I can remember correctly, old Charley went up to that gothic castle when he was here. He waited a while before enterin' that mansion though. He was more observant of the way things were goin' on in this township. Charley was more of an investigator but not the type that you may be thinkin' of, but that's a story for another time to talk about.

I think he knew there was somethin' not right about this township when he ended up here. It didn't take 'im too long to realize there ain't nothin' natural about them women all those years ago.

He did talk to a few folks who were still alive back then about this township of Sacrificale Grove and most of 'em didn't really say too much about what was happenin' around here 'cause they were too afraid of what would happen to 'em, but one person did speak 'is mind about them women and those monstrous kids.

That happened to be Clyde who spoke 'is mind and what he had to say wasn't too pleasin'. Old Clyde didn't give a rat's ass about what others may have thought.

After bein' here in this town for quite a while, Charley learned that them women left out of town on certain nights throughout the year to conduct their rituals out of sight from everyone except that one day durin' the late spring. He had noticed that they left out when the moon was showin' her dark side.

All the while that he was observin' them women, he was also observin' that mansion as well, and I do think that them women were also observin' him and knew what he was doin'. I was with 'im on occasion from time to time back then.

He noticed some strange things goin' on in that old buildin' which I think he wanted to check out. He never did get a chance to check out that schoolhouse though after bein' in that old haunt up the road from this mercantile.

Well, he sure did formulate a plan to go in that mansion when those women left out for their rituals. I think he told Clyde what he was gonna do as them two men had gotten together many times.

Well, Charlene, if you remember her, never did get involved with what Charley was plannin' on doin'. The only thing she mentioned was that the place had a dark presence about it.

Charley then bided 'is time after makin' 'is plans and observed the phases of the moon and when it was on the wane, he watched them women but not in a way to where it was obvious, but I think them women knew his intentions though.

When that moon showed her dark side them women and those children left out of town wearin' their robes they had always worn. Charley then proceeded to go on up to that mansion on up that hummock. He just about turnt around 'cause of how dark of a place that structure is and he felt the evilness of it, but he gathered his resolve and marched forward.

When he got up to the front entrance, he found that the doors to the place were left ajar a bit and as he peered in, all he saw was blackness. He looked back to where he had started from and had a view of the small town of what he could see that night.

He tried to see if anyone had seen 'im go up there to the mansion and when he couldn't see anybody out there anywhere, he slipped in through the openin'. That darkness enveloped Charley like a blanket and he could feel the weight of it.

He stood in the foyer while 'is eyesight adjusted to the gloom for a bit. As 'is eyes adjusted to the darkness he was able to detect recognizable shapes and objects but not enough to know exactly what they were. He had to feel around while navigatin' around the interior of the place.

He did manage to enter one of the rooms from the foyer and when he was feelin' around, his hands groped some object which he thought was a candle from the feel of it.

He later told Clyde that he should have brought a candle with 'im as he didn't know how dark the place was gonna be that night.

Well, luckily, he did have some matches on 'im as he was a smoker. His instincts were correct as he was able to get the candle lit, and from the bright glow of the flame he was temporarily blinded. He had to wait a bit while his eyes readjusted yet again.

He then proceeded to explore 'is surroundin's and went from room to room lookin' for some evidence, but only he knew what he was lookin' for.

Charley didn't say too much about what he found in that place except there were unspeakable horrors that no human should witness. He had found evidence of death, and the aroma was unbearable. A few of the rooms on the upper levels of the mansion had the tell-tale signs that death had occurred.

Charley had to be careful where he stepped as there were spots on the floor that were too weak to step on or had holes through the floorin'. There were many areas in the walls where the planks were exposed as well.

The basement level of the structure was more terrifyin' as the smell down there was horrendous, which made Charley gag. He did find somethin' that piqued his interest in the lower levels though.

All the while Charley was in that place, he swore that somethin' was watchin' 'im the whole time. He didn't know where it was or what it was, and the longer he stayed in there the more fearful he was gettin' and his nerves were gettin' the better of 'im. By the time he got to the basement he had no idea how much time had passed since he entered the place.

Whatever it was that Charley had found in that dark dungeon, he took it with 'im and he decided to depart the mansion as quickly as possible before them women finished their ritual and came back. It was a couple of hours before the sun rose from the eastern horizon when he left that house of horrors behind. As he was walkin' away as fast as he could, he could still feel eyes upon 'im as whatever it was, was still watchin' 'im.

Some of them women watched old Charley after that event and I do believe that those women knew that he had been in that desolate place. Margret Barlow, which is supposed to be Victoria's mother, really did watch him as if she disapproved of what he had done. Jennifer tried to get into his head quite a few times, but he avoided them women and those beastly children whenever he could.

Charley told Clyde of his harrowin' experience and what he found while he was in that old mansion. Charley then decided to check out that house on up the road from this here mercantile. I guess whatever he had found prompted 'im to explore that old haunt for a couple of nights. It is also the reason why them women back then berated 'im when he went snoopin' around where he really weren't suppose to.

Like I had said earlier, he never did get a chance to explore that schoolhouse 'cause before he died he went crazy mad after bein' in that old house just up in the woods north of the main road. So I suggest that you stay clear of that mansion that's sittin' on top of the hummock and don't let Ann or any of t'other women try to get you up in there or you may never come back out alive.

I'm sure you know that there ain't no church buildin' in this town or anybody preachin' out against them women. Come back tomorrow and I'll tell ya more about that. For right now I need my rest.

CLANDESTINE

Good for you to join me today. I was wonderin' when you would show up. I take it you're ready to hear another story of the history of this here place. Sit yourself down and get comfortable.

There ain't no church buildin' or any preachers here if you have ever noticed that while you've been here in Sacrificale Grove. There were some folks who thought that the schoolhouse was a church or could have doubled as a church at one time, but that's very unlikely as those evil tykes are there most of the time.

Don't get me wrong, there may have been a church in this township at one time or another but that must have been a long time ago. No one these days knows what had become of it though. If you ask me, I think that the old ruins that Charley stumbled across when he had spent some time at the old haunt could have been that church buildin'.

Whatever happened to that buildin' has to do with them women bein' in that town and possibly with that part of the woods north of here. Well, that's what Charley believed anyways.

As far as there's no preacher here in this township of Sacrificale Grove, there ain't nobody actively preachin' out against the damnation of them women and those children and what's happenin' around here. Oh, we had quite a few zealots durin' the time I've been here. How many before I came I'm not able to tell ya. Some of those folks were really freaked out and the way they put it was that Satan 'imself was in this here township. Some of those folks even tried to exorcise what they called the devil out of this place, displayin' their holy relics without any success.

Them women were not amused or even affected by none of that religious nonsense. Some of t'other folks stayed quiet but silently prayed to their God, but I believe that them women knew their thoughts though. Most of them young folks had met their end in terrible ways or ended up in those woods where that misty fog is.

No salvation this place is.

Some of those folks who had claimed that they were self-proclaimed prophets of their God had said that the church in the town had to have been corrupted the way things were goin' on in this here township. They had said that the church and the town itself need to be cleansed, if only that were possible. The only problem about what some of those religious fanatics have said about the church is that they didn't know this place had no church buildin'.

I remember one couple who ended up in this area many years ago. I believe their names were Eugene and Candice Harris. They were travelin' evangelists from the southern States goin' from town to town back then.

From what I understood, after they had finished with their revival and so-called healin' the sick and lame after a few days of their stay in one town at some church, they were headin' to another town to another church. They thought they had gotten lost on the road even though they had taken that very same route many times when those two ended up here. As they were travelin' on the road to get to their next destination, a swirlin' foggy haze started to build up and from what Eugene had said the fog got so thick it was like pea soup and he had to slow 'is car down to a crawl 'cause he couldn't see the road ahead.

He never noticed that they had gotten onto a dirt road until the vehicle they were travelin' in died on 'em. When he had gotten out to check on the darn thing is when he had noticed that the road became a dirt path.

Unfortunately there was nothin' he could do about gettin' that contraption goin' again, so the couple had decided to walk through that fog, and they had gathered what they could and set out but at a slow pace as it was very difficult to see anythin' up ahead as that fog was thick.

It took them a while to get through that unnatural fog and seemed like hours to 'em and before they knew it, the fog started to thin out and they were able to see a little farther in that swirlin' mist. Well, that couple managed to break free of that foggy curtain surroundin' this here township and I'm pretty sure they thanked their Lord and Savior for their deliverance. I don't know if they saw that sign off the side of the road but if they did, they weren't able to read what it says.

The first buildin' they saw was this here mercantile and when they got closer to it, they were able to see Jacobs Tavern off in the distance.

I saw 'em walkin' up to this here mercantile as I was sittin' right here on the porch like I am right now. They were clutchin' their books as if they were some holy relic. When they got up close to me, we had greeted and introduced ourselves to one another.

Eugene had done most of the talkin', sayin' that their vehicle had broken down on back down the road and they had to walk through some unusual thick fog just to get here, wherever this place might be. He also wanted to know if there was a telephone somewhere that they were able to use. Well, I told 'em about where they were, as in what township this is, and that there were no telephones nowhere around here. I also mentioned that there ain't no service station in this township either. I really don't remember where they were tryin' to get to as it's been many years ago, some time after Clyde had passed away.

By the looks on their faces I could tell they were in disbelief on what I had told 'em. They just had no idea how stuck in time this place is. I don't believe this township is anchored to the outside world like it's suppose to be, but there are doorways leadin' in to this place only, but not leadin' out.

Well, I said to the couple that if they may be stayin' for a while, that I was guessin', that there is Jacobs Tavern on up the road where they could get a room while they stayed here. They thanked me and as they were headin' to the town itself, I overheard Eugene sayin' somethin' about havin' a revival in this here township and with them endin' up in this here place must have been the Lord Almighty's plans for 'em. I didn't catch the rest of what they were sayin' as they were out of earshot.

One thing that was on my mind at that point was that there ain't nothin' good gonna come to those two, and it sure wasn't the Lord's doin' for havin' them here either, if you been payin' attention you know what I mean.

They did end up goin' to Jacobs Tavern and meetin' Jennifer who provided a room for the couple. I can't really tell ya much about that encounter, but soon after they had settled in their room they apparently decided to explore the town some or try to find the local church and pastor that is nonexistent here.

They went over the bridge and passed the blacksmith shop that weren't in use at the time and continued through the town without seein' anybody yet. They went off to their right after crossin' the bridge instead of goin' towards that novelty shop that's on the north end of the town. They stayed to the south end of which is where the few livin' quarters are located at.

The couple must have thought that the town was deserted for the most part 'cause of the state of decay of the structures at the time. It's also when they went to a few of the homes there were no answer at the doors when they knocked, and the few folks who were stayin' in some of those houses didn't open the door to reveal themselves.

Them two continued on hopefully to come across somebody or a church buildin'. Well, they did come across a structure with a door open and as the two got closer, they could see someone in the old buildin'. It appeared that the woman in there was workin' a turntable with wet clay on top makin' some sort of pottery. She had long flowin' dark brunette hair with smudges of the wet clay on her cheeks, brow and clothin'.

Eugene knocked on the door post to get the woman's attention and she looked up from her work, and upon seein' the couple clutchin' their holy books she may have looked like she was pleased that they had stopped by her place for their perspective, but far from it.

Her thoughts when she saw Eugene and Candice at her open doorway was that they were fucked; her words not mine.

Eugene introduced 'imself and Candice to the woman, and he tried to preach on to her about the good book, but the woman stopped 'im and told the young couple that there ain't no God in this here place, but they can try to convince t'other folks to the contrary but not her. She told 'em to go on about their way but to be careful on who they talk to around this here township.

Bein' a little offended and puzzled by what she said, the couple took their leave and traveled through the town up until they got to that old rundown town hall and constable's office. They did see that old mansion on up the hummock, which upon lookin' at it they were disturbed greatly as that place emanated a dark presence.

Few of the folks who were watchin' the couple from their homes saw that they crossed themselves when the couple saw that old mansion. Eugene and Candice talked amongst each other, probably along the line of cleansin' this place of unrighteousness and evilness and gettin' the folks of this township right with their Lord and Savior.

They did leave that area quickly, and as they were comin' up on the town common the couple saw the schoolhouse and thought that it was the town church buildin'. Just when the couple was about to go up to that schoolhouse, Margret Barlow, the name that Victoria had used at that time, stepped out of the buildin' with those kids followin' her. Eugene and Candice saw that the woman was wearin' an old-style dress like what women wore in the fifteen hundreds, or the sixteen hundreds. The reasonin' for that woman and those children comin' out of that schoolhouse at that time, I couldn't tell ya.

Eugene had asked Margret if the deacon of the church was available and that evil woman just replied coldly that there was no church and that which she had come out of was the schoolhouse.

Well, I can tell ya that them little tykes had a disturbin' effect on Candice 'cause they just stared at the couple while standin' out in front of the schoolhouse. The couple did leave from that area while lookin' back ever so often at Margret and them creepy children.

As they continued their little tour of the town, the couple spotted a woman who looked just like Susan Moore at Damnosus Gifts who seemed to be a little more approachable than some of t'other folks they had encountered. Eugene and Candice decided to go into the novelty store that's on the northern end of the town common where the edge of the woods is just on the back end of the shop. They did see the foot trail not too far from that buildin' leadin' into the woods which is close to those stables which the couple did notice off to their left as they approached the smilin' woman.

The woman that was standin' just outside of the gift shop introduced herself as Sissy Bachman but she is actually Susan. Don't ask me what them women's original names were as I don't know that. Samantha may be able to tell ya that, but it's unlikely as she holds many secrets and won't tell 'em which could be best for us regular folks, I'm thinkin'.

Sissy invited the couple into her novelty store to eventually get 'em to pick out one of those cursed charms that calls out to some of the young folks who get drawn into this township. When the couple followed her in and seen what was inside the shop they were stunned at what they saw. A lot of those young folks who had entered that buildin' said it was like bein' in a cult-worshippin' shop. Eugene mentioned that this township weren't natural at all and it was more like Satan's playground after seein' what he saw in that shop.

Candice crossed herself and said mostly to herself, "Lord Jesus save us."

Eugene spoke up and said that the shop and the town was an abomination unto God and the people needed to repent for their sins and ask for mercy from the Almighty to be saved from His wraith.

"How can your God be lovin' when He tortures and executes the innocent and you claim that it's His will but in reality it's man's will for such to be done as there is no God but somethin' made up to control the masses," is what Sissy said while lookin' at Eugene.

"Blasphemy! God's wraith will rain down upon you, sinner."

Just after he spoke that, Candice jumped back in fright and was stumblin' out the store 'cause she saw Sissy transformed into somethin' hideous lookin' like a rotted corpse and vampiric for a split second. The thing is Eugene never saw that even though he was lookin' at Sissy the whole time.

Candice must have knocked somethin' over while she was retreatin' out of the buildin' 'cause Eugene turnt around and saw her leavin' out quick. He left givin' chase and caught up with Candice as she was half walkin', half runnin' passin' the stables. She didn't want nothin' to do with this place at all after seein' what she saw, but the young evangelist convinced her to stay sayin' that they were meant to be here in this township.

He was sayin' that it was God's plan for 'em to be here in Sacrificale Grove and to cleanse it from the wickedness and exorcise the demons out. It was God's way of testin' 'em.

Eugene had no idea how wrong he was, and Candice was a fool for believin' in that bullshit. They may have been able to convince the folks of other places they been to of their ability to drive out made-up demons from others but not in this here place.

The couple ended up goin' back to Jacobs Tavern where Jennifer offered 'em a plate of food and comforted the two young folks, especially Candice, sayin' that they must be exhausted from their trip and was only imaginin' things that weren't really there and that the next day would be a little better. That woman sure did get in their heads 'cause their minds were a little more at ease after that.

Don't believe they had a peaceful night's sleep though 'cause they had a haunted look in their eyes the next day. They may not have been able to remember what they had dreamt, but they knew it was disturbin'. Nonetheless, they pushed through with their faith and set about to spread the good Word to the folks in town. They decided to go back through the residential area again as they didn't want another chance encounter with those women and kids.

Instead of goin' door to door to spread the Word, the couple went to the center, or as close to the center of the residential area as possible. Once there, Eugene started to preach loudly so that the folks in their homes would be able to hear what he was sayin'.

After Eugene was preachin' for a while about them townfolks turnin' to Christ and Salvation and talkin' about exorcizin' the evilness from their lives and castin' out devils and demons in Jesus's name, a few of the folks looked out of the homes they had claimed to look upon the couple; a few of them folks stepped out their doors a little. Somethin' that them townsfolks noticed was that while Eugene was preachin', he never did open that book he had in his hands to read none of the scriptures from it, but instead waved it around, shook it at them folks and thumped on it at times.

It wasn't long that some of the folks were startin' to come out of their homes of which Eugene and Candice had thought they were comin' out to hear the Word better. Mayhap a few of 'em wanted to hear what he was sayin', but some of t'others were lookin' out for one of them demonic women to approach.

He was so good at what he was preachin' about and how he was preachin' it that a few of the folks thought that Eugene must've been a Savior sent to deliver 'em from this nightmare that they were in. Candice was in agreement of everythin' Eugene was preachin' about, and the couple called a lot of the townfolks their brothers and sisters in the Christian faith.

At the end of the Sermon the couple greeted some of the folks and those who greeted them two evangelists put on a somewhat nervous smile whereas t'other folks went back in those old houses not wantin' to do with what was goin' on anymore.

As the couple was leavin' to go back to the tavern, Candice caught sight of one of them women standin' off in the distance toward the eastern part of the town, lookin' toward the young couple. That made Candice a little nervous, but she kept it to herself not tellin' Eugene about it.

Well, Jennifer catered to the couple that evenin' as well and all durin' their brief stay here in this township of Sacrificale Grove. Do believe Jennifer played along with what the couple were doin' in the town and got 'em to believe that they were makin' progress.

The couple didn't get that much rest that night either from the disturbin' dreams they were havin' but still couldn't remember what they dreamt, and even the next night after that and the next. It was really affectin' Candice 'cause each day she was forcin' herself to smile as the days went on.

Each day they went back to where they been goin' to preach onto the folks of the town and some of them were startin' to be taken in by the couple, especially Eugene just from the way he spoke. That woman Eugene and Candice had met while she was workin' her pottery came out and listened for a while but went back to her abode shakin' her head at the nonsense that was goin' on.

Each day that Eugene held his sermon, one of them women was always seen off in the distance to the east lookin' out toward the couple.

If I could remember correctly one or two of those damnable creatures that are the women started to mess with those two young evangelists. I think it was Ann, although that wasn't the name she was goin' by at the time, who was messin' with 'em, or it could have been one of t'other women.

The woman came up to the couple after a few days of them preachin' to the townsfolks claimin' that she was bein' possessed by evil spirits, but she did give a look to t'other regular folks to keep 'em silent of what she really is. Them folks backed away and a couple of 'em went back into their homes not wantin' to be a part of what was about to transpire.

That evil woman begged and pleaded with Eugene to rid her of that evilness that had possession of her. He was taken aback by this unexpected news but, thinkin' that he knew what he was doin', proceeded to exorcise the so-called demon from her with him layin' his hand on her forehead and prayin' to his God to shine His light upon her and in Christ's name demandin' the devil to come out of the woman.

I believe he was only puttin' on a show at first 'cause he must've done it many times before on others as just an act for the congregation of the churches them two had been to with the help of someone who was also in on it, but he seemed to falter a little when the woman's face changed a little to more of a demonic vampire or some other hideous monster from nightmares. Her face didn't change fully as it still resembled her features as bein' someone normal.

Eugene was still goin' at it but he seemed to be a little nervous by then at seein' what he saw for the first time. A few more of the townsfolks left 'cause they didn't want no part of what was goin' on. Very few of the newer folks who were allowed to live here in this township stuck around to see if exorcisin' that woman would work, as Eugene seemed to be a prophet of God to them folks as they thought that he might lead 'em out from this nightmare they were in.

Candice backed up and crossed herself when that woman's face changed, frightenin' the girl a lot as she had seen Sissy's face transformed back in that novelty shop.

After a while Eugene had to stop as sweat was pourin' out of his body. He said that he had to take a break and would continue the next day if she would return. Actin' like she was tired herself from the ordeal, that woman agreed. They continued for the next two or three days thereafter.

Durin' that time and the end of the so-called exorcism, guttural sounds started to come out of that woman's throat that no sounds should come and she started speakin' in a dark demonic voice cussin' the young pastor. Eugene was taken aback as he had never heard nothin' like that before in his whole life. He had asked and pleaded with God for a divine intervention, while shakin' with fright. On the last day of the exorcism at the end of it when he said, "By the power of Jesus Christ, I command you to be gone," sayin' it rather forcefully and loud, the woman's face turned back to normal and she dropped as if she fainted.

Fakin' like she was a little faint, the woman slowly got up and had thanked Eugene while he helped her up and said somethin' about the novelty shop bein' an evil place and that was where she was at when she felt like she was possessed by somethin'. Then she said that he should do an exorcist rites on that place which she then took her leave sayin' that she had to go and had thanked 'im again for what he had done for her.

Eugene told her before she left that he would, as that woman got into his head, but he needed some time to rest before he even attempted the endeavor. The few folks who stuck around and saw what happened agreed that he should do somethin' about what was happenin' around this township and started to believe that God had bestowed onto Eugene gifts to drive out the evilness from this place. They had also believed that the woman was exorcized of the evilness about her and she was then just a normal person just like them, but that belief didn't last too long though. Us older folks knew better.

What them folks who witnessed the recent events didn't know was that it didn't really work 'cause as that vampiric woman was leavin' she had a smirk splayed on her face as she was walkin' away from the young couple and the townfolks.

Before Eugene and Candice left to go back to Jacobs Tavern for the night, he told those few who stuck around that he would do what he could the next day and offered a prayer before departin'.

The couple had another fitful sleep that night as well and, for Candice, she seemed to have been caught in a continuous nightmare durin' those nights she's been there as she was lookin' a little ashen and her eyes were always wide open, dartin' to and fro, and she was beginnin' to be spooked quite easily. She had been clutchin' her holy book even tighter since that event with that supposed possessed woman.

Eugene did promise her that he would be by her side to protect her from whatever may come their way, and that she should be behind him so that she would be safely away from bein' harmed.

The next day they left out of the tavern and started into the town, crossin' that bridge spannin' Hallow Creek and was about to head towards Damnosus Gifts when a few of the townfolks met them on the town side of the bridge. A lot of t'other folks stayed back in their homes as they knew nothin' Eugene did would work in this place, even if he or Candice may have believed it.

That woman who been doin' pottery forced her way up to the couple and told 'em that they had no idea what they were dealin' with as she had enough of the bullshit that was goin' on for the past few days. Those creatures masqueradin' as women had powers clandestine and what the couple were doin' and kept doin' meant nothin' good would come of it. If they wanted to save themselves, they would stop at once, but they can keep at it if they want, it was their choice.

That was the only warnin' the couple were given by that woman, and with that she left and never interacted with the two after that.

Candice became apprehensive about everythin' she thought she had believed in about her faith and may have thought of not continuin' on, but Eugene convinced her what they were doin' was the right path as that was God's plan for 'em.

Couple of the folks who had met 'em that mornin' encouraged the couple to do somethin' about that novelty shop and exorcise the evilness from there. Some of t'other folks nervously agreed to that, but t'others had second thought after that woman gave Eugene an earful.

Eugene got Candice to continue on towards that novelty shop with 'im as they held onto their holy books but none of t'other folks followed after 'em as some didn't want to get involved and they prevented t'others from goin'. Apparently, a few of the older folks had a talkin' to some of the newer folks the night before for them to leave well enough alone.

Nonetheless, the couple went on up to Damnosus Gifts, and when they were approachin' the store, those damnable kids were standin' outside of the schoolhouse watchin' the couple.

Don't think Eugene ever saw what Candice had seen when they saw those children. To her those faces on them tykes changed to some kind of beasts she couldn't describe and changed back to what they were before real quick. She wanted to turn around and head back the way they had come right then and there 'cause she stopped in mid-stride, but Eugene urged her on and said that it was God's will that they must go on no matter what. It was more like he wanted to keep goin' 'cause he felt like he had somethin' to prove for some reason.

Well, she reluctantly followed him up to the shop rather nervously bein' real close to Eugene, and he brought out his holy relic, it bein' a cross, and held it before 'im as the couple got to the entrance of the gift store. The door to the place was opened as if it was invitin' the two in and Eugene went in first brandishin' his cross in one hand and holdin' onto his holy book in the other. Reluctantly Candice followed right behind.

It didn't take long for their eyesight to adjust to the dimness of the interior to which they spotted Sissy, as you know she's really Susan Moore, near the back of the store, standin' in front of the counter.

"It's nice of you to come back and visit my little shop again. How has your stay been in our little town?"

"You will not tempt us, spawn of Satan. The power of Christ compels you."

"Oh, please. Why don't you pick a gift of our gratitude and generosity? You know it calls to you," Sissy said, and she moved a little closer to the couple, and it seemed like she floated instead of takin' a couple of steps toward 'em.

I think to believe she was talkin' more to Candice about takin' a gift than to Eugene, 'cause later Candice found out she had taken a charm of some sort from that place without even realizin' it.

"Stay back! We will not take nothin' from this accursed place or accept anythin' from the likes of you. You and your kind are an abomination, for the power of Almighty God commands you," Eugene said.

"You honestly believe that the trinket you holdin' will protect you from us? I think not as it's a made-up concept that man came up with," she said, laughin' a little afterwards.

"Vile wicked creature, you will not beguile us with your lie, for Satan himself is the lord of lies. Go back from where you came and leave this place at once for Christ commands you." While he said that, Eugene took a step toward Sissy, boldly thrustin' his cross before 'im.

Sissy laughed at the absurd remark Eugene made, then said "Foolish little man, you people always associate your beliefs with ours and force it in like a puzzle piece that doesn't fit with a nearly completed puzzle. Your Satan has nothin' to do with us as he is just made up to suit your purpose."

"Lies! You are a liar!"

Sissy then, with swift quickness, closed the gap between herself and Eugene and grabbed a hold onto the cross he was holdin' and snatched it from his grasp, cuttin' him with her long sharp nails. Her features changed to somethin' more hideous, somethin' dead, but yet alive, and when it opened its mouth, Eugene could see sharp teeth in its maw, and the thing's eyes became black as coals and there was a foul stench about it. Candice screamed and was out of that buildin' before she knew it. The townsfolks did hear that scream that had come from Candice even though they were some distance away.

It seemed like Eugene froze for a second or two before he managed to stumble backwards and head out the doorway, trippin' over his own feet. When he got outside and looked about to see where Candice was at, he spotted some sort of beast among those kids near that schoolhouse that he had never seen before. It and them children were just lookin' toward his direction, and there were laughin' comin' from that gift store behind 'im.

He did manage to find Candice headin' toward the bridge really quick just passin' the stables, and he took off runnin' to catch up to her. He caught up to her fairly quickly and when he lightly grabbed at her, she cringed from 'im and told him that she wanted to leave from this place immediately. She pleaded and begged to get away from this township, and she wasn't able to take it anymore about how this place is and the way some of the people are here.

That last incident had scared her so bad that she was shakin' with fear. Oh, Eugene did relent and agreed to leave but he persuaded her that they would leave first thing in the mornin', which she didn't want to do at first but leave right then and there. After some persuasion from Eugene, she finally agreed to head out in the mornin' after they try to get some sleep that night in their room at the tavern.

They headed back to Jacobs Tavern and went straight to the room they had been occupyin' durin' their stay. The couple didn't fare too well that night, and I do believe Candice had a very nightmarish dream that night which was worse than the previous nights before. The next mornin' some folks who were new to this place heard screamin' comin' from the room Eugene and Candice were stayin' in.

As it turned out, Candice woke up to a bloody mess with Eugene torn to pieces in the bed next to her. Jennifer conveniently showed up in the room to give comfort along with a couple of those other women, which one of 'em may have been Ann.

Well, Jennifer had those two women take Candice out of Jacobs Tavern, but that poor girl had no idea where she was bein' led to as she was in a catatonic state of mind. Jennifer reassured t'other guests that things were alright and had 'em go to the common room downstairs and made sure they didn't see the carnage in that room.

Them two women just about half carried Candice through the town on towards that mansion while the townsfolks looked on through the windows of their livin' quarters. No one ever saw Candice after that day when she was bein' escorted into that dark structure sittin' on top of the hummock. You can probably guess what happened to her.

As for the room that the couple occupied, it's been cleaned up as if nothin' ever happened. Whatever Jennifer did with the body, no one knows.

***

Derrick, if you remember him, was a devout Catholic when he was younger. That was before he ended up here in Sacrificale Grove.

Just before bein' drawn to this place, he was questionin' his own faith and had doubts from what he said. I think he was tryin' to be a priest or a pastor at one time.

Derrick ended up bein' drawn into this township well before Rowland came here, that's if you remember him, and seemed to be a lost soul in search of 'imself. From what he had said, he was transferrin' 'imself from the church he had been with for many years to another in a different city.

Apparently there were some allegations that was brought up that made Derrick needin' to separate 'imself from the corruption that he had no part in, and he was havin' some trouble with his faith prior to that, but that scandal was a tippin' point for 'im.

As he was drivin' to his destination, without thinkin' about it, Derrick turned off onto an old back country road. Before he realized what he did, thick foggy mist was formin' all around 'im while he was travelin' on that road. As you know, his vehicle had shut down which meant he had to walk the rest of the way as he was unsuccessful gettin' his vehicle goin' again. He noticed that the road wasn't paved like before and it wasn't long till he came out of that fog and came upon Thomas Mercantile and saw me sittin' on this here porch.

Just from the way he was dressed, I could tell he was a clergyman.

He had asked me what town he was in and I told 'im of which I also warned 'im not to take that old dirt road that led up to Clyde's old shack as it dead ends about a mile up there.

He told me that he had a bit of car trouble and I told 'im that there weren't no one around here who could help 'im with that, but there is a place he can go if he needed somewhere to stay while he was here. I do feel sorrowful for directin' folks to Jacobs Tavern knowin' how that place is. It's not like that the townsfolks will bring someone in who just got to this here township knowin' how some of those damnable women are.

He then asked me where the church was located as he felt that he would be able to stay there more easily of which I told 'im that there weren't no church anywhere in this town and haven't been for many years. He was a bit puzzled by that comment and said that every town has at least one church in it. I replied kindly, "Not here, and if you're here long enough, you'll find out why."

Bein' a bit confused by what I just said, he continued down the road to Jacobs Tavern and acquired a room there quite easily as there really was no one else who showed up except that he met Ann there. She had said to 'im that she thought she was the only person who was new to this place until he showed up, but you and I both know that's bullshit.

After securin' his room, Ann convinced Derrick to explore the town of Sacrificale Grove and he agreed to that. When they left the tavern, she led 'im across the bridge and instead of goin' towards the homes which were off to their right, they went up towards the novelty shop and the common.

Ann commented on how old the buildin's were but Derrick noticed that quite a few had some work done on 'em. They got to the common without runnin' into anybody and by that point Derrick was wonderin' if the town was abandoned. That was when Susan Moore stepped out of Damnosus Gifts but he never did see her as he was lookin' somewhere else.

Ann told Derrick that there is someone else here in the town and pointed towards Susan, which Ann got 'im to check out that store.

He had an uneasy feelin' about the place when he entered the shop. Susan welcomed the two into the town, even though she knew all too well about Ann. She then offered Derrick a gift of 'is choosin' but he declined as he felt very uncomfortable about the whole place and didn't want to stay in there any longer than he wanted to.

He decided to leave out the store and when he did, he noticed them kids out in the school yard. He must've thought that if this place had a school, why didn't it have a church? By the time he finished that thought Ann showed up and got 'im to go with her on towards the old constables' office and the town hall without givin' those kids a second glance. Derrick wondered if Ann even saw those kids as she never did look their way.

Derrick went with her as he wanted to put some distance between him and that gift shop, and he also wanted to get away from them creepy kids, as he found it a little disturbin' the way they just stared at 'im.

When they got to the town hall, Derrick felt some sort of presence weighin' down on 'im and he didn't like the feelin' of it. It felt a little dark to 'im and he couldn't figure out where it was comin' from. It was when Ann, in her chirpiness, pointed out the mansion up on the hummock that he found out where that dark presence was comin' from. Well, she tried to get 'im to go with her to check out the old place and he told her no and that he didn't feel too good, so he left and instead of goin' back the way they came, he decided to go through the residential area of the town.

After walkin' a bit, he heard a woman's voice sayin', "You might want to be careful of who you hang around with, preacher."

That startled 'im from his thoughts and he turnt around to where the voice came from to find out who spoke to 'im and saw a woman 'with long flowin' greyin' black hair standin' in a doorway of which he replied, "What are you talkin' about?"

"Some people around here are not what they seem," she said and nodded in the direction where Ann was standin' as she didn't follow Derrick but stayed rooted where he left her watchin' 'im walk off none too pleased. When Derrick looked back at where he was earlier before takin' off, he saw Ann turn around and walk up to the mansion, but for a brief second he thought he seen that girl floatin' as if she was a specter.

"Like I said, some people are not what they seem."

Just before that woman who spoke to Derrick went back inside her abode, he said, "I was told that there isn't a church here."

"No, there ain't and if you're able to stick around long enough, you'll find out why."

With that she disappeared in the confines of the buildin' leavin' 'im standin' there thinkin' that someone else had told 'im that same thing earlier.

Derrick decided to head back to Jacobs Tavern as the events of the day left a lot for 'im to think about and try to make sense of all the confusion.

He didn't fare too well that first night stayin' in that tavern just like t'other folks before 'im as he had those disturbin' dreams like everybody else has when they stay there.

Derrick did come back to this here mercantile the next day; I'm guessin' to seek me out.

"There's somethin' wrong with this place," is what he said to me when he came up onto this here porch.

Yep, I was sittin' here when he came up, like I always do nowadays.

He then said, "You know what's going on don't you?"

"Ayuh."

"You people are part of a cult aren't ya?"

"It may appear to be so, but believe it or not there are some folks within the town are still holdin' on to their beliefs as Christians even after what they had witnessed. Some of t'others lost their faith. It's some of those women you want to watch out for."

I then told 'im about some of t'other folks who ended up here where faith was different than some of t'others, and some of 'em I couldn't understand what they were sayin' 'cause they were speakin' in a different language I didn't know nothin' about. Some were German, others were French, whereas many others were from some other country I didn't know about and couldn't tell ya where they were from. Well, anyways, we had a little talk, Derrick and I.

Derrick did fine while stayin' in this town and he did get to know a few of the townsfolks like Frank and Patti. He tried to avoid some of those evil women and I got to say, he did a fairly decent job at that.

With everythin' that had happened while he's been here he questioned himself on whether or not God even existed and questioned his own faith even more.

There's been many newcomers who ended up in this township durin' the time Derrick has been here and some of 'em he met, but while he may have seen 'em one day, the next day they weren't around anymore. He did see a few of 'em go off into the woods north of here but they never returned. A few times a body was found in them woods and a couple of 'em, give or take, were someone Derrick had just met who had been drawn into this place. He may have had a thought about leavin' this town from all that was happenin' but he kept seein' one of them women watchin' 'im for a while before goin' about their business.

Derrick did have a chat with the woman he had met the first day he came here some time later. She was workin' on some pottery at the time he decided to talk to her, which she's been doin' for most of her life.

"Nothin' in this place bothers you does it?" he asked her as he looked in while the door to her place was wide open.

"I see you managed to last this long, priest, and no, nothin' does. I've been here all my life. What's on your mind?"

"Many people who come here leave, that's if they haven't been killed, but whenever I think about leavin' out of this town, they're always watchin' me. Those women I mean."

She chuckled a little then said, "Nobody leaves this place. You'll find that out the longer you're here. Ever figure out why there's no church yet."

He told her that he may have an idea why but wasn't quite too sure considerin' what he had noticed durin' the time he been here and asked about what she meant by nobody leavin' this place, but she never answered his question.

He had been sensin' some odd vibes while he had been chattin' with her and said that he had to go and so he went, leavin' her to her pottery. He couldn't explain what it was though.

How he managed to survive the winter here, I couldn't tell ya. Mayhap he has a strong will to live and a strong mind.

Derrick did tell me at one time that perhaps what the church taught 'im was complete bullshit and that God never existed and everythin' that's been happenin' here in Sacrificale Grove was reality. He couldn't speak for everyone but for 'imself. How could he have faith in somethin' that didn't exist? Oh, he has plenty of faith in 'imself though. I didn't say too much, but mostly listened to 'im as I thought he just needed someone to talk to who didn't creep 'im out.

Now, this 'talk' we had was some time just before Rowland ended up here in this township. Well, I shouldn't have to tell ya what happened when Rowland was here as I've already told you that story.

It was after them vampiric women had their sacrificial ritual that Derrick decided to try to leave from this place headin' through the woods to the south. I shouldn't have to repeat that story either as I have already told ya that one too some days ago.

Derrick is still around, and I'm sure you ran into 'im on occasion. He has no belief in the good book anymore or in the church, but that's just him. I can't say the same for everybody else around here though.

Nowadays, in some ways, he's almost like what Clyde use to be. He has gotten a little harder around the edges since his return from tryin' to leave this place.

If you had paid much attention to what I told ya when you got to this place, you may have some inklin' of why there ain't no church here or no one doin' any preachin'. Oh, there are a few who end up here and start preachin' the Word from time to time. Nothin' good comes of it though.

This is the end for today. Be sure to be here tomorrow as I'll tell ya about that schoolhouse you've been anxious to hear about. Until then, I bid you good day.

THE SCHOOLHOUSE

Well, I see that you're already here. Been waitin' for me have ya? Give me time to settle in. Damn my old bones. Let's get to it shall we?

I'm sure you have been curious about that schoolhouse for a while. As you know them weird kids mostly congregate in the school yard. I'm pretty sure you've seen 'em already. No one really knows what's in that buildin' except for maybe a few of the regular folks.

Victoria been in there many times as well as some of t'other women. Ann Price does mention that schoolhouse sometimes to the new folks who end up here, that's if she's pretendin' to be a newcomer when those young folks end up here in Sacrificale Grove. She somehow gets into a few of them folks' heads for 'em to try to sneak into that schoolhouse without bein' seen. Oh, some of 'em do go up there but most of 'em don't come out. Only if two or more go in there then mayhap at least one may come out alive.

One of the normal folks in town was out doin' somethin' one evenin', can't rightly recall what that person was doin', when one of them foolish folks came runnin' out of that accursed schoolhouse. That there person who was mindin' their own business doin' whatever it was they were doin' went up into the nearest buildin' and hid quick like when they saw the person come runnin' out of that schoolhouse.

That townsfolk peered out the window and what they saw was that young folk ran close to where they were hidin' before one of those beasts took that fool down. Then out of nowhere another of those creatures joined t'other and they tore into that young fool while they were screamin' for help. No one came though. Then those things dragged the person off while they were screamin' for somebody to help 'em. The screams died off in the distance and the person who witnessed what happened didn't come out of their hidin' spot till the next day.

There has been one person who I have known many years ago. She came here about the same time that Charley did and from what I understand she went into that old schoolhouse some years after she got here, at least that's what Charley said anyways. Her story of how she came to be here is a story for another time. She was a unique person I have to say.

Like I said before, Charley was gonna check out that schoolhouse but he died before he could do that. I believe Clyde tried to warn 'im about not goin' into that old haunt just up the road from here.

There was one such person who went up in that old school some years ago and she made it out alive and told me in secret of her experience.

I have never told anyone about it for many years but I guess I'll tell ya.

Her name's Vicki and she claimed to be a self-proclaimed psychic before endin' up in this here township. She sure did figure out that she could manipulate others and make a livin' off of it. She told me the tricks she uses when she did that. She convinced t'others of her 'ability' to communicate to the dead and bein' able to read minds. She would ask generalized questions like a common initial of a person's name and let them folks fill in the blanks and some of the stuff she said, she would get right. It was more like parlor tricks than anythin' else, usin' magic props of the mind. It was like doin' a cold readin' of how she put it.

Then she started to have strange dreams and visions that she never had before. She could never understand what they meant and those dreams were startin' to affect her 'performance'. Durin' her wakin' hours she would have visions, even durin' her 'readin's'.

Well, she was booked to a 'readin' in some town and while she was drivin' she made a turn on an old country road. She couldn't explain why she did that when she weren't suppose to.

She traveled down that road a good ways before she started goin' through some thick misty fog. Shortly after, her vehicle had shut down on her and she wasn't able to get it goin' again so she got out and started walkin', which led her to this here township.

Vicki got to Thomas Mercantile after passin' through that fog, and upon seein' the store she thought she had seen it before but wasn't too sure about it.

I wasn't sittin' there on the porch when she first got here but she did go up inside and met Samantha's mother, Charlene, of which Charlene had known that the girl had some sort of 'talent' about her.

When the girl asked about the whereabouts she was at, Charlene told her that she was in Sacrificale Grove of which Vicki didn't know anythin' about this place and she just knew that the town shouldn't be here at all.

As if readin' the girl's mind Charlene said, "No, it shouldn't be here but I should warn you, be careful who you talk to as some people here are not what they are. If you get a chance get with a man named George."

Vicki did notice that the store didn't have any modern appliances that were common to her timeframe while Charlene was talkin' to her.

Not really knowin' what the woman meant and bein' a little weirded out, Vicki excused herself and left out the store. Once outside, she looked up the road and saw Jacobs Tavern in the distance sittin' next to the bridge spannin' Hallow Creek. She decided to walk on up to the tavern up the road to see about gettin' information from someone who didn't weird her out.

It wasn't long after she started walkin' that she stopped dead in her tracks. She had sensed somethin' that was just off to her left and when she looked to the woods to the north, she wasn't able to see anythin' that disturbed her but birch trees, a few evergreens and bushes. She knew there was somethin' in the woods that was hidden and she thought it best not to go there to find out what it was. Not able to figure out what it was she kept goin'.

When Vicki got to Jacobs Tavern she looked out across the bridge and saw other structures as well. She stood there for a moment debatin' on whether or not she should go across that bridge to t'other side of Hallow Creek. Somethin' was tryin' to draw her across that bridge for some reason but she was a bit nervous about goin' so she decided to go on in the tavern.

When she went in the tavern it seemed empty of life. Off to her left, there was a fireplace with no fire goin' and to her right was a flight of stairs leadin' up to the upper level, and scattered throughout the common room were a few tables and chairs. In front of her was a passageway leadin' to the back to what she assumed to be the kitchen area.

Vicki stood there really not knowin' what to do for a bit before one of them women showed up, but it wasn't Jennifer. The woman told Vicki the proprietor of the establishment was out and wouldn't be back for a while but she said that she could help out whatever Vicki needed help with.

Vicki asked the woman if there was anybody who could help her with her car as it had broken down on her on the road a few miles back. The woman said that there wasn't of which Vicki then realized she had seen the woman before but wasn't able to recall from where. Mayhap from one of her readin's she had done in the past maybe.

The woman said that she could get Vicki a room if she needed it. Not knowin' what else to do, Vicki accepted the room, which the woman showed to her and said her name was Sarah and if Vicki ever needed anythin' to not hesitate to ask, then Sarah left Vicki to herself.

Not wantin' to be stuck in her room for the rest of the day, Vicki decided to go back down the stairs to the common room. Once there she saw Sarah sittin' at one of the tables with another woman. Sarah introduced the other woman to Vicki and said that she had just got into this town as well and her name was Vivian, which was the name Ann went by back then.

"It's crazy how that fog was isn't it?" Vivian said to Vicki.

"Yeah, it sure was. Did your car break down too?"

"Why, yes, it did. Do you want to go out and check out this place?"

"Sure, I don't have anythin' else to do."

It is strange that when Ann Price meets the newcomers at Jacobs Tavern and pretends to be new herself, no one ever sees her gettin' a room there.

Well, Vicki and Vivian both left out of the tavern and crossed that bridge to t'other side of Hallow Creek. Instead of goin' to the right where the homes are where the regular folks live, Vivian took Vicki off to the route up to where that novelty store and the schoolhouse is at.

As they were walkin', Vicki started to have a vision of an interior of some buildin' and there was a person standin' near the back, but there was somethin' wrong about it. The person didn't look quite human but Vicki wasn't able to get a clear view as the vision was distorted some.

When Vicki came to her senses, she noticed that she had stopped walkin' and Vivian asked her if there was somethin' wrong. After standin' there for a bit, Vicki said that everythin' was fine and she was ready to keep goin'.

They continued on up the road until they got to the common not that far from the novelty store. Vicki then had another vision where she was somewhere underneath some buildin' in what looked like a basement and there inside she saw some sort of beasts that she couldn't describe, eatin' on somethin'. When she came back to herself, Vicki was starin' at the schoolhouse not knowin' why.

"Are you sure you're fine?" Vivian asked.

"Yes, I'm fine."

"Well, let's check that place out. The door is opened," Vivian said, as she was referrin' to that gift shop on the north end of the common.

Vicki agreed with her and they went into that buildin', and the interior of the place looked very similar to what Vicki saw in her vision, but to the back of the shop she saw Sissy Bachman. It had come close to the vision she had seen and she was thinkin' to herself that it was strangely weird.

"Welcome to Sacrificale Grove. Would you two care to pick out a gift of our generosity of your choosin'?" Sissy said, knowin' that Vivian wouldn't take nothin'.

Vicki looked around the store then said, "I don't think so, I feel sick." She then bolted out and threw up on the ground beside the buildin'. Apparently with them women tryin' to get in Vicki's head had made her nauseous somehow.

Vivian stepped out the gift shop and asked Vicki if she was ok and Vicki said that she wasn't. Vicki then said that she was gonna head back to the tavern and get some rest and hopefully she might feel better later on.

Vicki started walkin' back, but on the way, she had a sensation that somethin' or someone was watchin' her, so she turnt around and saw Sissy standin' just outside her shop next to Vivian, lookin' at Vicki, then she saw them kids outside the schoolhouse starin' in her direction. She turnt back around and quickly went to the tavern and to her room.

When Vicki finally managed to fall asleep, she had a dream which the thing about that was, she was able to remember what she dreamt. In the dream she was inside a buildin' that resembled an old schoolhouse and there was somebody with her. Even though she couldn't tell who exactly it was, she knew it was a man, with him in front of her.

Next thing she knew, she was underneath in a basement of some buildin' with the same man. He was in front of her the entire time. Then there were some short figures there ahead of 'em and they seemed to be those kids she had seen earlier. All of a sudden, they changed into somethin' beastly and at that moment the guy turnt around and grabbed Vicki by her blouse and flung her to where those beasts were and he ran away. Just when those creatures pounced on her is when she woke up.

She laid in bed for a moment thinkin' of the dream she had. It was just so vivid she couldn't make sense of it. When she rubbed her face, she found that she had sweated durin' her sleep.

She gotten up and went down to the common room and it was there she met the proprietor of Jacobs Tavern, which happened to be Jennifer. Vicki didn't see Vivian at all.

"I had heard that you had gotten sick yesterday. Are you doin' much better?"

"A little better, yes."

"You're not with child, are you?"

"No, I don't think so. I mean I haven't been with anybody in a while."

Jennifer knew that Vicki wasn't pregnant but she did know that there was somethin' about Vicki. I believe Jennifer knew that Vicki somehow became an actual psychic and not a fake like she had been. What Jennifer didn't know was how that happened.

Vicki then had decided to go out to get some fresh air. Once outside she looked up towards Thomas Mercantile then out across the bridge. She was thinkin' about comin' to this here mercantile but somethin' was callin' for her on t'other side of Hallow Creek.

Feelin' like she was bein' pulled to the bridge, Vicki went across it and as soon as she got to t'other side she was met by Vivian.

"Oh, hey, you feelin' better?" Vivian asked.

"Yes, I had to get some fresh air after sleepin' in that stuffy room."

"Oh, that's good. I was out earlier this mornin'. There's somethin' you ought to check out with me."

Then there was a flash of a vision that Vicki saw of a large structure that she couldn't make out too well as there was somethin' ominous about it. Somethin' dark. Then a voice that Vicki heard in her head said, "Don't enter. It's death for those who do."

When Vicki came back to herself, Vivian was lookin' at her and there was somethin' in that woman's eyes Vicki didn't care for.

It seemed like Vivian was sayin' somethin' to Vicki that she couldn't quite make out so Vicki said, "What did you say?"

"You spaced out for a second. Do you still wanna go and check this thing out with me?"

Sensin' somethin' sinister, Vicki said that she would think about it and that she was gonna walk through the area she hadn't been, such as to say the residential area, and asked Vivian if she wanted to join.

"Well, maybe later then. There's somethin' else I want to do."

As Vicki was walkin' away she had a strange feelin' about somethin', and when she looked back she saw Vivian standin' where Vicki left her, just lookin' at her. Vicki was thinkin' that this place was weird and there was somethin' wrong with some of the people here and couldn't understand why Vivian didn't want to go with her.

Still havin' the urge to be somewhere, Vicki kept goin' and she passed some of the old homes which she had no idea that a few of 'em was occupied. The townsfolks never did come out to greet her and the homes looked so old to her that she didn't think anyone lived in 'em.

When she got to one of the structures, she stopped without really knowin' why, and then a woman came out of that buildin'.

The woman had long flowin' dark hair and she looked at Vicki for a while as if studyin' her. Before Vicki could say or do anythin' the woman said, "You're not like the others who end up here. You're different."

"How do you mean?"

"You've been havin' visions," the woman said as it really wasn't a question, but more like a statement of fact.

"How do you know that?"

"I know things most people don't."

"I don't understand this. I've never had this before."

"No, you haven't."

After doin' a little thinkin', Vicki said, "You must be the only one in this part of town. I haven't seen anyone else besides those who I have already met. There are only women here and they're kind of strange, though."

"Oh, there's others here, and not just women. They just rather not get involved with anyone who is new to this place. Not after what happened to a preacher and his wife a few years back."

Havin' the feelin' that not knowin' what happened was the best for her, Vicki… was in a room lookin' at a young man and woman lyin' in a bed asleep. Then a smoky haze came through the bottom of the door to the room. It started to gather near the bed where the girl was havin' a fitful sleep.

That haze was beginnin' to take shape and formed into a figure that resembled a female wearin' an old Victorian dress. It looked to the sleepin' girl for a while before it transformed back into a smoky haze of which it then entered into the girl through her nose and partly opened mouth.

When that smoky haze had completely went into the sleepin' girl, she drew in a deep breath and her eyes opened wide, which they seemed to be completely white.

Then a strange thing happened that was not possible for anybody to do. The girl rose up from her prone position in a straight posture onto her feet with no assistance from herself or anyone else. Her nails grew into sharp talons and her face became twisted into somethin' hideous and monstrous as she rose from the bed.

She then turnt around without movin' her legs or feet and looked down at the sleepin' young man for a second or two then with one swipe of her talons she sliced the man's throat nearly decapitatin' him. There was gurglin' sounds comin' from the man as he was tryin' to breathe without any success and his eyes opened to see the creature, just before it tore into him.

After the carnage had been done, the thing slowly fell onto t'other side of the bed, layin' back down, and as it did the features changed back to what the girl looked like before. Then that smoky haze came out of the girl through her nose and mouth as it had entered, and formed near the bed becomin' that same female figure.

It looked down upon the sleepin' girl for a moment before it turnt around and seemed to float towards the closed door and as it did its head turned to face Vicki.

That womanly figure never did open the door but passed through it as if the door wasn't even there.

Vicki was then lookin' at the woman who had been talkin' to her before she found herself in that room with the sleepin' couple. She was breathin' hard as if she was hyperventilatin'.

"What did you see?" the woman asked Vicki.

"He was torn to pieces in the bed while he slept."

The woman just nodded in understandin' and said, "Have you met a man at Thomas Mercantile when you first came here?"

"No, I haven't."

"He goes by the name George. He's usually sittin' on the porch of the store. You should talk to him. Tell him Heather sent ya."

"Somebody else told me to see this man George. I think I will."

Without another word, Heather went back into the buildin' she had stepped out of when Vicki stopped by there. Well, if you were wonderin' what her name was, that's it.

Thinkin' it over for a moment, Vicki decided to head on back over to Thomas Mercantile. She left and went back to the way she came and, on the way, she noticed someone lookin' out a window who quickly disappeared out of sight. Well, Vicki really didn't think nothin' of it and kept goin'.

When she got to this here mercantile, I was sittin' here but I wasn't here when she first got here as I was doin' other things. Anyways, she came up to me and asked if I was in fact George and I told her that I am. She then told me what had happened to her recently, while she was sittin' next to me. I suggested that she should heed her visions as they may come to pass, but she may be able to change the outcome of what they show.

She told me that she had a room at the tavern but she didn't want to go back there at all. I didn't ask the reason why 'cause I had figured that it was the way the place is. I told her that she could stay in the guest house out behind this mercantile and she accepted the invitation and she been stayin' there durin' her time here.

For the next couple of nights Vicki had those dreams; still with the same guy, still in the same buildin', still the same outcome. She had also dreamt of that woman she had seen in her vision in the room with the couple. That woman was always seen just outside that schoolhouse in her dreams.

One day a young man ended up here and I watched 'im walk up the road to this here mercantile. When he got here, he told me that his car had broken down in some fog down the road. I told 'im that I was sorry for his inconvenience but there ain't nobody here who could help 'im with that. Then he asked about a phone that he could use and again I said there weren't any around here. He thanked me for my time and proceeded up the road towards Jacobs Tavern. He seemed to be a bit confused by what I told 'im when he left.

Vicki came around and asked me about the guy after she saw 'im walk away. I said that I didn't know anythin' about 'im of which she said that she recognized him. That subject was never brought up again after that.

Vicki ended up goin' back into the town when she ran across the young man as he was just about to go across that bridge. When he spotted her, he said, "Well, hello there."

"Hi."

"Would you care to join me? I was about to go on up to this place I was told about."

"Umm, I don't know."

"Come on, it looks like you could use some company."

"I don't think so, I'd rather not. We just met and I really don't know you."

As it turned out, he convinced her to go with 'im. They walked up to where that novelty shop is, and once there she refused to go in with him even after he had asked her to. She stated that she had already been in there but he tried one more time to get her to go in with 'im. She still refused and he ended up goin' in by 'imself.

As Vicki watched 'im go in, Margret Barlow, who is really Victoria, stepped out of the schoolhouse, and not long after them kids came out. Vicki had the distinct feelin' that she had seen Margret before just from the way that woman was clothed in a Victorian-style dress. Vicki thought that Margret was that woman she had seen in her vision she had a few days ago, and in her dreams.

After a while, the young man stepped out of Damnosus Gifts and he noticed Vicki lookin' towards the schoolhouse and those kids. He saw 'em standin' in the yard starin' in his direction. Then Margret led them kids away from where they were off towards that mansion.

"What's that?" the man asked, pointin' out the buildin' that the woman and those kids were leavin' from.

"I believe that's the schoolhouse."

"Kind of small don't you think? Looks like one of those that you might see in an old western town maybe. But it's much older. It could be a church though."

"No, it's a school."

"Maybe we ought to check it out."

"I don't think so. Someone might see us go in."

"We'll go when no one is around."

"I don't know."

"What are you afraid of? I'll be with you."

With a little proddin' he got her to agree on goin' in the school durin' the evenin'. They decided to walk around to pass the time and while they were walkin' they were lookin' at t'other old structures and when they got to the jailhouse, Vicki felt a strong dark presence whereas the guy didn't.

They walked on a little until they saw that mansion up on the hummock. That was when Vicki realized where that dark presence was comin' from.

The young man tried to get Vicki to get a little closer to the place but she declined sayin,' "There's somethin' wrong, I don't feel too good. I've got to go back."

"What's wrong?"

"I just don't feel good."

They started headin' back the way they came, but just before leavin' Vicki looked up at the mansion and she thought she saw one of them women standin' at one of the windows of the place. It must've been Vivian or Sarah but Vicki wasn't too sure about it. But she started to feel a little better when they left the area.

When they got close to the schoolhouse, they cut across the common and went to the stables and the blacksmith. They had spent very little time in the tool shop as there really weren't that much to look at, but they spent quite a while up in t'other two structures that they almost lost track of time.

Just before dusk the young man decided that it was time for both of 'em to head over to the schoolhouse, but Vicki was a bit nervous about it 'cause all she kept thinkin' about was that dream she been havin'.

When they got to the schoolhouse the guy looked around to make sure nobody was watchin'; of course I believe them women knew what was goin' on though. The door to the gift shop was closed and there weren't anyone in sight.

He checked the door to the school and found it to be unlocked then proceeded to open it; the young man entered first and right behind 'im came Vicki. Within they saw a few desks and chairs or benches of which most of the furnishin's was broken.

As they proceeded through the buildin' Vicki had an eerie feelin' that it was just like her dreams she had, with him bein' in front of her with everythin' lookin' very similar.

As they got further in, he pointed out that there weren't no chalk boards anywhere.

"For it suppose to be a school, there's nothin' in here that indicates there's any teachin' goin' on," the young man remarked.

They got to t'other end and he said, "There's a stairwell here. It must go down to the basement."

He motioned Vicki to follow 'im and she reluctantly followed 'im down the stairs knowin' what might happen next. She was thinkin' in her mind that he was gonna throw her into the midst of those creatures just to save his own skin.

They got to the bottom of the stairs and it was a little darker there than it was above. They let their eyes adjust to the gloom before goin' on.

The man led the way and again she was struck with how familiar this was to her. They could smell how musty it was and there was another aroma down there as well. It smelled like somethin' was rottin' somewhere down there. To Vicki it was like death was in the air.

They picked their way in the gloom with him leadin' the way. They didn't get far when about two or three of those children materialized out of thin air in front of 'em. Vicki didn't see it happen but she heard the guy say "What the fuck?" She then looked ahead of 'im and saw those kids.

Then that vision flashed before her of him grabbin' her by her blouse and throwin' her towards the kids while he was tryin' to get out.

When she came back to her present situation those kids changed right before their eyes and became some sort of hairy beasts. Vicki wasn't able to describe what kind of creatures they were but they seemed to be a cross between a feline and a canine from what she could see in that gloom.

Then it happened. The terrified man turned around and tried to grab at Vicki and knowin' how it was suppose to have played out, Vicki dodged his advance and forcefully pushed 'im when he lost 'is balance and stumbled.

She didn't see what happened after as she was runnin' for the stairs. She did hear 'im scream in pain and agony as she was climbin' the stairs to the floor above. Once she got to the top landin', Vicki didn't stop; she kept goin' and left out the buildin' quick.

When she got outside, the sun was just dippin' below the western horizon and she kept runnin' and never stopped until she got here to this mercantile. She may have looked back once to see if anythin' was comin' after her of which there weren't.

When she passed Jacobs Tavern, she thought she had seen Sarah standin' in the doorway with a smile on her face watchin' Vicki run for her life.

Needless to say, Vicki never did venture out ever again. She never did try to leave this place either and as she put it, there's a ring of that mysterious fog surroundin' the township of Sacrificale Grove and nobody ever gets to t'other side of it and they seem to be stuck in there with no way out. There are some folks who do end up comin' back though, mayhap some weeks later or months later, just like Derrick did.

Vicki is still here but she tends to stay in the guest house mostly.

It seems that the schoolhouse is used more as a den for them little bastards than anythin' else.

Old Charley had said at one time that he had seen one of them women take somethin' into that old school. That was when he was observin' those women before he went into that mansion. He didn't know what it was but he knew that there was a person who died up in the woods close to that old haunt just up the road. Don't rightly remember how they died though, but like I said, Charley saw one of them women takin' somethin' into that schoolhouse shortly after that person had died.

Well, that's all I have for ya. Feel free to give an old man some company any time. I don't know if I'll have any more stories to tell; maybe, but I doubt it. If you will excuse me, I'm gonna go get some rest.

www.ingramcontent.com/pod-product-compliance
Lightning Source LLC
LaVergne TN
LVHW011838060526
838200LV00053B/4083